BEFORE THE SNOW

THE GREATEST GIFT SERIES
BOOK ONE

JENNIFER HARTLEY

Jennifer Hartley

My Gift For you

Get your FREE Copy of "Back To You " Today!

Enjoy!

CHAPTER 1

C armen looked away from the angry faces of the four men glowering at her as they stood surrounding her desk to take a sip of water. It looked like she was gathering her thoughts. Partly. It was more of a delaying tactic because she is fucking didn't know what to do.

Bands had volatile members and even more volatile relationships. Such groups came together bound by idealism and pure love for music, leading to deep friendships. Fame, however, had a way of destroying what they had worked so hard for. Lots of things sprang from fame. A member was more popular than the others, often the singer, and given more opportunities. There was also the problem of record companies dictating their sound, leading to lawsuits that dragged on for a long time. Drugs, women, men, and constantly on the road took their toll.

Seismic seemed to be above that. When Carmen first discovered them, their sound was a harsh yet melodious metal that drew blood from the ears and made the heartbeat so fast as if it was racing towards death. It was a sound that gave the finger to end proudly.

The seismic frontman was Ramiro Brandt. His angel-blond hair was up to his shoulders. His bright emerald eyes and elegant, chiseled features looked perfect whether he was onstage wearing only his sweaty abs and fitted, ripped jeans or at an award show in a tailored tux. He also played the lead guitar. Rhythm guitar and backing vocals were Lennon, the exact opposite of Ramiro in looks with his harsh, cruel-looking features and oft-unkempt iron-black hair. He looked terrifying in a leather vest and pants, and the most flattering description of him in a suit was that he looked like an undertaker. Lucas Atkinson was the bassist and also did backing vocals. He had a grim face - one journalist joked that he looked like his entire family had been wiped out in the most horrible, and just found out he had cancer in one day. He was already balding at thirty-seven and looked to be ten years older. Their drummer was Russell Leblanc, more pretty than handsome with his dark blond curls and lopsided, teasing grin that was said to melt the knickers off women. Euan Estrada, who played the keyboards, rounded up the group. He was said to be as good-looking as Ramiro, while some believed him to be more handsome. His hair was a rich, pale blond that he wore past his shoulders, and his eyes were big and soulful.

Seismic was the biggest rock band of the decade, and Carmen was determined to keep it that way. She had been babysitting these assholes early on, but the problem they had come to her for was something she couldn't fix. It made her want to throw things. Nothing was impossible with Carmen Schwartz, but the problem of Ramiro Brandt was making her question that. It had been going on for a while.

"He's been slacking off practice and getting high for days," Lennon growled, planting his vast fists on the desks and glaring at her accusingly with his pale gray eyes. "We're recording an album in three months, and that fucking twat has not turned in any material." They all wrote songs, and each of them contributed as expected. It was their way of holding off the record moguls from touching their sound.

"He tells us he's sick, but this is what he's been doing." Often calm, with a Zen-like demeanor, Euan slammed a folded newspaper on the desk and jammed his finger on the headline. Carmen winced as she read it: `Beast Bows Before Vodka' was plastered on the front page along with a photo of Ramiro passed out in front of a bar.

"I'm not saying the twat has no right to get wasted," Lennon continued, "but if he keeps this up, we're kicking him out."

Carmen paled. "Y-You can't be serious." Her blue eyes were giant pools of disbelief and shock as she stared at each of them. They all looked her right in the eye without blinking. "You can't be fucking serious!"

"Carmen, this has been going on for a year. Look, we understand that it was an awful way to lose his sister like that but come on," Russell said. "The god cursed me because you shouldn't speak ill of the dead, but Temperance Brandt was an evil bitch, and she was so demanding of Ramiro. There," he told the rest of the band, puffing up his chest as if in a challenge. He was the shortest in the group. "I said it. Temperance's a bitch, and I'm glad she's dead."

Carmen silently agreed. Temperance was Ramiro's sister. She was beautiful in a way that made the heartache and cruel in such that she crushed the spirit. Brother and sister were close, but she was a little too possessive. She sneered at groupies who approached Ramiro and cut down any woman who showed even the slightest interest. She and Carmen had had shouting matches as well. Temperance that Carmen was going to steal Ramiro away from her. Carmen didn't know where she got that idea. She was hardly the kind of woman Ramiro would look at also had never had any interest in Ramiro except professionally. Yet Temperance considered her a threat and threatened to kill herself if the band didn't fire Carmen. Ramiro defended Carmen, the only time he went against his sister.

Carmen had no love for Temperance Brandt, but that car accident was not how she should have gone. It was too quick yet still cruel.

"I disagree about kicking Ramiro from the band," Lucas said. "But Carmen, you have to understand. We're becoming a joke because of

3

him. He's late for shows; he's grumpy and rude. He's getting drunk and high all night. I don't care what the man does in his own time as long as it doesn't affect the time for the band."

"He's right," Euan said. "We've worked too hard to lose what we have."

Again, Carmen agreed. But seriously? Did they want to kick Ramiro out?

"I understand your sentiment - "she began.

"Oh, fuck sentiment!" Lennon howled. Lucas elbowed him in the ribs. "Will you shut up and fucking listen? Go on, Carmen."

"But people have a different way of mourning. You can't kick this guy when he's already down. And may I remind you that Ramiro Brandt is why we're all in this room, living where we live, having what we have. He put up the band and discovered each of you. He wouldn't be here if you were in his shoes, telling me this unfortunate thing about kicking him out. Maybe instead of uniting in your impatience and frustration, you should be at his side helping him."

"He's not answering our calls or messages," Russell pointed out. "No, Carmen. You're the only one he'll listen to."

Carmen shook her head. "I don't know him as you do. You're his best friend! I'm. . . I'm your manager."

"Oh?" Lennon crossed his arms. "Are you saying you're no friend of ours, eh? What are we, money pots for you, then?"

Blushing, she protested, 'I didn't mean it like that - "

"Sure sounded like it."

"Definitely." Euan agreed, his gaze sharp.

"What I *meant* to say," Carmen snarled, "is that I don't have the kind of friendship with him that you have. For crying out loud, you all went to college together. You were fucking roommates!" She pointed at Euan. To Lennon, she added, "He paid for your rehab!" Glaring at Lucas, she said, "He introduced you to your wife! And you - "she told

Russell - "who gave you a place to live when your family cast you out because you're gay?"

"SHAME ON ALL OF YOU," SHE YELLED AT THEM AS SHE STOOD UP IN HER heels. "for coming here to *my* office, telling *me* that you intend to stab Ramiro in the back, your friend, your friend who has fought and helped *each of you,* and then demanding that I *do your fucking dirty work! Fucking blockheads, the lot of you!*"

Carmen was so furious at the conspiracy they wanted her to be a part of, of the betrayal they had been planning. A bitter taste at the back of her throat threatened to choke her.

The men had shrunk back during her outburst. They looked at each other before turning back to her. Carmen was still red-faced and fuming, her fists clenched to her sides. Betrayal. It was disgusting. It so went against her principles, yet here they were, the band she admired, asking her to destroy them. Ramiro Brandt was infuriating, and his actions of late, she had to admit, were no excuse, but neither was their decision. How could they easily forget that it was Ramiro's songs that won them awards, that he was the emotional center of their group? And they dared to call themselves his friends?

"So, uh, Carmen," Lennon said, clearing his throat. "What do you think we should do?"

RAMIRO LIVED IN A FIVE-THOUSAND-SQUARE-FOOT PENTHOUSE. THE doorman greeted Carmen as she nodded at him. She got on the elevator reserved only for Ramiro and his guests, fortunate enough to have the passcode. After punching in the four-digit code, the doors opened. It was a quick, smooth ride, with the elevator opening at the penthouse.

Carmen was wearing only a light, pale blue sweater because the weather was warm but with calm winds. The temperature in Ramiro's place was arctic. Her nipples tightened painfully, and she crossed her arms, looking around.

The interior designing to reflects tastes and sensibilities that were not Ramiro's. Temperance? Carmen wondered. She had been here many times, and yet this knowledge, nor her familiarity, gave any comfort. The dark, wooden divisions that reminded her of claws seemed ready to gouge at anyone walking close enough. The carpet that hushed her footsteps were the bright crimson of blood. It was sunny outside, yet it was dark and forbidding, unwelcoming.

"Ramiro?" She called out, still hugging herself. She had given him a heads up of her visit, and, as the guys had said, he took her call. She kept walking and looking around, peering inside rooms. She knew this place like the back of her hand.

When it was clear he was not in any of the rooms, she took a deep breath and knocked on the red-lacquered double doors leading to the main suite. She listened for a bit, then pushed them open.

Sprawled with abandon in the middle of the bed was Ramiro.

Naked.

Carmen gasped and quickly averted her eyes, swaying on her feet. As she righted herself, her hand brushed on a wine bottle on the table, and it fell, crashing into pieces on the floor. "Fuck!" She whispered, looking frantically at Ramiro, who was stirring and smacking his lips. As she turned to get out, her hip hit another table. A pained yelp escaped her as she doubled over and tripped on more bottles on the floor.

"Carmen?" A confused-sounding Ramiro demanded. "What the fuck are you doing here?"

Her cheeks the color of beets, she whirled around and shut her eyes. "Ramiro, for the love of God, will you put some clothes on!"

"Oh, please. It's nothing like you haven't seen before," he drawled.

"Ramiro!"

"Alright, alright," he muttered, and she imagined him rolling his eyes to the ceiling and shaking his head. Her eyes still closed, she listened to him shuffle, the bed squeaking as he left, hopefully, to cover up. He was taking too long. Hand over her closed eyes, she demanded, "Are you decent?"

"Well, I'm covered, but I don't know about being decent." There was a brittle edge to his voice. She opened her eyes and turned to him again. He had put on a cheesy, dark red robe with black piping. He was hungover because he struggled to remain on his feet, and his stare was blurred and unfocused. He sighed and sat down at the foot of the bed. As he did, the robe parted, and Carmen again had to turn away.

"Ramiro, if you could shut your legs, please."

"God, what is this - the mighty Carmen is a prude!" Ramiro exclaimed. "You've seen cocks before, Carmen." But as she turned to glare at him, he crossed his legs. "There? Better?"

Carmen gestured at the bottles on the floor. "Did you empty your wine cellar?"

"I tried."

"That's not wise, Ramiro."

"Funny you should say that. My brother Robin has always believed that drinking brings knowledge." He looked at her in a way that had her arms wrapping around her chest. "You could use a drink or two."

"Be serious. I'm here to talk to you about the band."

Ramiro looked bored. "What do those cunts want now?"

"Those cunts are your friends, and they're concerned about . . . "she stared at the bottles and then at him. "Your behavior."

"My behavior."

"You're due at the recording studio in three months, and you still need to give them something. Are you going to write something or not?"

"Are you asking as my manager or as my friend?"

Carmen put her hands on her hips. "They're worried, Ramiro. Getting smashed and high aren't exactly productive."

"No," he agreed. "But then I don't hit the bottle because I want to accomplish anything worthwhile."

"Then why?"

"Why?"

"Yes. Why?"

"If I'm able to answer that, what will you do? Haul my fucking ass to AA? Lecture me like you're doing now?"

"Whatever it takes to get you back on your feet."

"And writing and recording and singing. Fuck that. I don't care anymore."

"Ramiro - "

This time, he leered at her. Carmen would throw one of the bottles at him if she were at the breaking point of her temper. She knew he was trying to intimidate her. So she stared back at him, disappointment all over her face.

"Ramiro," she tried again. But he shook his head.

"I'm not in the mood for lectures or anything that has to do with the band. I will rather be left alone if you're not going to lose that nice sweater and kiss me and fuck me."

"You're drunk," she told him. "And you sound like an idiot."

Ramiro's smile was mean. "That's the nicest thing anyone has said to me in a long time. Get out of here, Schwartz."

There was no reaching him. She gave it to him straight.

"The band saw me and told me they want to fire you. They wanted me to do it, and I told them to go fuck themselves. I'm here because I believe in you, Ramiro. At least, I did until a few seconds ago. I came here to talk to you, help you if you let me. Since that's not going to happen, I'm leaving. I can't watch you destroy yourself. It's too painful."

Ramiro went back to bed. "Fine. Go. That's what everyone does, anyway."

Carmen watched him curl on his side and draw the blanket over his head. Then she turned on her heel.

As she grasped the doorknob, Ramiro spoke.

"No one's getting rid of me. I quit."

CHAPTER 2

 *ne year later*

RAMIRO BLINKED AS THE TOO-BRIGHT CAMERA FLASH LASERED RIGHT into his eyes. He rubbed his eyes as he was led away toward the jail cell. No handcuffs bound him anymore since he had become a frequent visitor of police stations within a hundred-mile radius of his house. He still had to be fingerprinted and photographed. Still, the police officers were friendly and even offered him a cup of coffee before subjecting him to the dull, tedious process.

"Why are you on duty tonight?" Ramiro asked the officer guiding him. He was an awkward, fat guy with cow-like dark eyes. His badge read Keith. "Isn't it your wife's birthday?"

"I took Rita out to lunch earlier," Donald Keith replied as he opened the steel door. "She understands. We'll celebrate this weekend."

"You should take her to The Platinum Bar," Ramiro said as he entered the cell and stepped away for Donald to lock him in. "She seems a special girl."

Don blushed. "She is. I'd like to, but you must reserve for months in advance."

Ramiro waved his hand, the motion lost. "Allow me to make the call. They always have a table for me."

Don looked flabbergasted. "Really? That's really nice of you, Mr. Brandt." He smiled hugely. "Wow. If you could, please. That's - Rita would love it. Thank you."

Ramiro lowered himself gingerly onto the bench. His steps were wobbly, but his mind was still quite clear despite the breathalyzer indicating his alcohol level was well over the limit. "As soon as my rescuer picks me up, I'll call them."

"Thank you, Mr. Brandt. I'll look out for your lady friend." Don blushed suddenly. "I mean, she's always coming for you."

"She's a loyal employee, nothing more."

Don waved goodbye, and Ramiro leaned against the wall, closing his eyes.

It would be a year since he told Carmen he was quitting Seismic before they could kick him out. He regretted the decision shortly, but he stood by his word. Seismic was his life, but there was nothing he could give to the band anymore. There was nothing to sing about or write about. Even his voice was off though Carmen told him it was because he smoked and drank too much.

The media ate up Ramiro's desertion of the band. They weren't too far off when they speculated that his erratic behavior led him to leave the group, but they were wrong in saying that he was forced to leave. Nobody forced Ramiro Brandt to do anything. Unfortunately, that was the general consensus, and he was too tired and angry with how things were to issue a statement in his defense.

He decided to leave the band, which he thought would please everyone. Instead, it brought down on him such savage wrath from everyone. His father, who never approved of his golden boy quitting school to scream onstage, declared that he had wasted the last twelve years of his life. Robin thought he was an idiot to still mourn over their bitchy sister and sacrifice his career. "The only thing in this world you loved aside from Temperance," he told Ramiro mockingly.

Lennon, Euan, Lucas, and Russell never spoke to him, but they made their displeasure known. They called Ramiro an ingrate, a self-centered asshole who made selfish decisions without consulting them. That was funny, considering they wanted to kick him out. They should be thanking him for sparing them the effort. An article was written about the feud and titled "The Clash of Beasts."

Ramiro continued drinking and getting high. Hardly a week passed when he wasn't pulled over, and the cuffs slapped on him. His lawyer Scarlet Gunn used to bail him out. Still, he got tired of her lecturing him that if he continued with this, he would spend some hard time in prison or, worse, actually end up hurting somebody. That's how people talk to him these days. They either told him he was garbage or shit.

Except for Carmen.

During a terrible night, he yelled out her name and digits when the police officer asked who to call for his bail. Ramiro had not seen her since she walked in on him in his birthday suit. He blamed it on the flashing red and blue lights of the sirens that reminded him of her eyes and her freckles. He must have passed out because when he came to, the jail cell was being opened, and he was gruffly told that Ms. Schwartz had paid for his release and was waiting for him.

That first time she came for him, she looked mighty pissed and uglier than usual with her messy, stringy hair, rumpled t-shirt, and jogging pants. She had clearly been asleep and forgotten about looking presentable. Their eyes met, and she shook her head at him.

Ramiro gave no thought to other people, but something about the resignation in her eyes got to him. He wasn't arrested for two weeks after that. Her shadowed blue eyes haunted him. When he couldn't take it anymore, he checked out his wine collection and hopped behind the wheel. His erratic driving led to his subsequent arrest.

He gave Carmen's name again.

Like before, she came.

She always came.

She always came and would only look at him, never saying a word. After assessing that Ramiro was alright, she indicated with an incline of her head that he followed, and he did. More silence followed in her car, a sensible, boring sedan. She started the car only when his seatbelt was on. She drove without another word nor even a glance at him. That was alright. Ramiro didn't want to think about her ugly face when he crashed on his bed following that, but those blue eyes started in his dreams.

Carmen Schwartz was not Seismic's first manager. The first was a sleazy, sweaty guy named Ramiro, who had already forgotten. He got the band gigs but in places where people were too drunk to realize they were there. After two years of that hell, they parted ways. The next few months saw them performing sporadically, but they managed to get regular gigs in better places. Places where people listened. Carmen went to those.

At the time, she was a shop-girl at a furniture store, going to school off and on because money for tuition and books wasn't regular. Her failure to provide a permanent address in the city prevented her from getting a scholarship. She stood out for Ramiro because she was often the tallest in the room at six-foot-three. Her hair was stringy pale blond, and the cheap makeup she used was quick to melt away and reveal her freckles. Her nose was big and crooked, broken during a mugging attempt the first time, and failed the second when an abusive boyfriend hit her. She had a full, thick-lipped mouth. An ugly freak, that's what she was.

Yet, when Ramiro would sing, he was electrified by the sight of her moving and swaying with the music. She stood near the front, ignoring the howls of disapproval because she was blocking them from their view of the band. The music and Ramiro's voice seemed all that comprised her world. When she would open her eyes at the end of a song, they were revealed to be the most transparent, striking blue he had ever seen.

"Great job," she would tell them as they were packing up then she was off. Sometimes, it was, "That was phenomenal," before disappearing again. She appeared in nearly all their gigs, wherever it was. She always knew the bartender, owner, or somebody of importance in those places.

Four months after Seismic were on their own, Ramiro broached the idea of hiring a new manager for the band. "Carmen Schwartz," he told them.

"You mean the tall broad, always high around us?" Russell said doubtfully.

"I mean the one who's always on first-name and repeat customers of the places where we perform," Ramiro said, not liking how Russell described her. He actually thought Carmen moved quite gracefully. "I can't be the only one who's noticed? She knows people."

"I heard she's got a lot of contacts," Lennon agreed. "Really into networking and stuff. Quite smart for a shop girl."

Ramiro gave him a warning look. "Hey, this person, I believe, would be committed to the band. Maybe we can give her more credit?"

"Ramiro," Lucas said, "I'm not saying the girl is an idiot, but you've seen what she looks like, right?"

"Nothing that a decent haircut and makeup won't fix," he said impatiently. "And you're the one to talk. Have you seen your receding hairline?"

"I may be getting bald, but I'm not ugly."

"I have old, muddy shoes that look better than you."

"Funny," Lucas said sarcastically. "A Brandt with old shoes?"

"So she knows people," Euan brought the subject back to Carmen. "But we need someone who's both a pit bull and a bloodhound, Ramiro. I don't know, but something about her tells me she's... timid."

"Let's see if she's willing and if it will work out. Anyway, we can always fire here if she fucks up."

Carmen Schwartz was not timid. She had the foulest mouth on earth, in Ramiro's opinion. Lennon was the champion of cursing, but Carmen outmatched him and sometimes made him blush. She was a bloodhound, sniffing out bullshit and opportunities to elevate the band's growing success. A pit bull, she wasn't, but a jackal - careful and more dangerous.

Under Carmen, Seismic not only got more and better gigs, but they also landed their first major record deal. They hit gold, as well as in their choice of manager. As Ramiro was famous for his outrageous antics onstage, so was Carmen's reputation. She told the greedy record executives to fuck themselves in the ass if they thought of screwing the band from their profits. One magazine put them on the cover and titled it "The Beauty and The Beast." Ramiro was smiling, golden, handsome, and clearly captioned as the Beauty. At the same time, Carmen wore her signature scowl and was labeled the Beast. Neither had posed nor given an interview for the magazine.

Ramiro and the rest of the Seismic thought the title was insulting. However, it praised him and Carmen for "taking the music back for musicians everywhere." They issued a joint statement denouncing the magazine's choice of how they portrayed Carmen on the cover and demanded an apology. They did, but Carmen would later tell them they shouldn't have bothered. "I'm used to it," she told them in a tone that conveyed further questions would never be entertained.

When Ramiro told Temperance about this, his sister smirked. "She's right. You shouldn't have bothered."

Carmen arrived at the station two hours later. Ramiro was annoyed because he wanted to go home and rest in bed. She had never taken this long before. Don again brought him to Carmen, who had just finished filling up the paperwork. Ramiro was ready with a smile, expecting her usual silence.

With hands on her hips, Carmen growled, "Until when, Ramiro?"

She usually picked him up with messy hair and one side of her face lined with sleep. Ramiro enjoyed that, knowing he had dragged her out of bed. This time, she wore a little black dress that showed off her toned, muscular arms, gym-honed body, and unbelievably long legs. She was not curvy - the dress's neckline showed no cleavage, but his trained eye caught sight of her tight nipples - but hell, she looked magnificent.

Despite having more alcohol than blood in his system, Ramiro felt his cock twitch.

"She speaks," Ramiro announced grandly to the police officers. Smirking, he strode toward her. "I thought you'd gone mute, Schwartz. How many times has it been - "

"Ten times. Ten fucking times I've come here to get you. Every time I thought it would be the last. That you're going to pick yourself up and get fixed. Instead you just get worse and worse." In her fury, Carmen's cheeks were the color of plums. She grabbed Ramiro by the arm as soon as he was close enough and yanked him out toward the night.

"Let go of me," Ramiro demanded, quickly shaking her away. He glared up at her. He was tall, but she was taller than him barefoot. In her high heels, she loomed over him.

"Seriously, Ramiro, until when? What the fuck are you doing with your life?" Carmen continued as they stood in front of the police station.

"You know, I liked you until you started speaking."

"I've hated you since the day you quit."

Startled at the venom in her delivery, Ramiro could only watch as she turned away and stormed to her car. Any other day would have him amazed that she could walk steadily in those impossible heels and endless legs. He watched, stunned, as she got behind the wheel. Seeing that he was unmoving, she yelled, "Get your ass moving or I'm leaving you, Brandt!"

He was still drunk but made it to the passenger seat just as she floored it. Ramiro clipped on his seatbelt and glared at her.

Carmen glared at him with fiery blues, then turned her attention back to the road. "I swear to God, Ramiro, if not for recent developments, I'd drive us off a cliff because I can't stand how you keep doing this to yourself."

"Recent developments? You mean you in a dress?" Ramiro glanced appreciatively at the smooth expanse of pale, freckled thigh exposed. "You look so fucking fetching."

"God damn it," Carmen swore.

"You know, I don't know if anyone's asked you this, but who the fuck do you kiss with that mouth?" Ramiro drawled. "It's *so* fucking filthy."

"Ramiro, do me a favor and just be quiet while I drive. And think."

She sounded like she was near tears, so Ramiro did as asked.

She pulled up right across his building ten minutes later. Ramiro would generally get out and never look back. This time, he remained in his seat and stared at Carmen. She was slumped in her seat and looking straight ahead.

"What happened?" He asked her gently.

"Do I . . . I mean, by not saying anything, by just picking you up after another arrest, am I encouraging you somehow?" Carmen looked at him, her expression helpless and frustrated. "What happens when you're prosecuted, when you actually have to spend time behind bars? You might not care, Ramiro. I shouldn't anymore." She shook her head and collapsed back in the seat. "That day you told me you were quit-

17

ting meant you don't care about anyone. Yet here I am. Another thankless night with you."

She sounded both angry and sad but still blunt. Damn, but she knew just how to cut him even when that wasn't what she meant to do. Carmen Schwartz was a hardass, but she wasn't cruel or unkind.

"For the record," Ramiro began, "I am grateful for what you do for me."

"What exactly do I do? Because if this keeps up I'm an accomplice, Ramiro. And I refuse to be part of whatever you're doing to hurt yourself even more."

"I'm not hurting myself," he snapped.

"No? What you're doing certainly breaks the heart." She retorted.

"What brought this on?" Ramiro asked. "You've never spoken before. Tell me."

Carmen looked at him, her lower lip trembling.

"I can't have any more nights like this, Ramiro. You're beginning to scare me. I just . . . I can't reach you. I can't help you. You're going to have to help yourself." She sighed. "I'm sorry. I'm rambling."

"No, not really," Ramiro said sarcastically, and she glared at him.

"The reason that brought this all on." She sat up slowly. "Okay. I guess it's something inevitable. I've been as patient as I can for you. I haven't seen even the slightest change in you, Ramiro. No attempt at anything to stop yourself from getting drunk and making an ass out of yourself. And I realized that I really can't be a part of something that will destroy the man I used to admire and worship. God, Ramiro, I don't think you know just how glorious you sound, how much of a gift it is and that it really breaks the heart how you're throwing it away. Me picking you up, bailing you out, I can't do it anymore. I'm sorry. But unless you make changes, I'm not going to be in your life."

Ramiro felt something in him die at her words.

Chewing her lip, Carmen continued, "There's also the fact that I just got engaged." She showed him her finger, and a small diamond ring gleamed. "I eventually said yes. Do you know why it took me hours? Because I kept looking at my phone, thinking there will be another call from the station and I didn't want to ruin it when Tanner asks me by telling him, `Got to go. Ramiro Brandt needs me.'" At his skeptical look, she blushed. "Ramiro, it's sick how it seems my life is revolving around you. That's why I'm putting the brakes on." She shook her head firmly. "No more nights like this. No more getting you from the station. No more getting my car professionally cleaned because I swear to god, Ramiro, you fucking stink of alcohol and cigarettes. I have a good life ahead of me and it doesn't involve you. This . . . you," she gestured at him loosely. "You're not the Ramiro I know. So I'm going to cut myself off you while I can still remember how you used to be, how good you were until . . . "she shrugged. "Everything."

She let out a sigh. Obviously, she had been controlling herself from saying these for a while.

That dead feeling still nagged from deep inside him. Looking at her profile, Ramiro pleads, "Carmen, please."

She shook her head.

"I can't not have you in my life."

He only meant to say them for the sake of doing so, but he realized as soon as he spoke it was the truth.

Carmen looked like she was going to cry. "I don't want you in mine."

CHAPTER 3

T wo weeks later

Since getting engaged, Tanner has been spending more time at Carmen's place. He had broached the subject of living together six months into their relationship. Now it was one year since he first brought it up, and Carmen was nowhere near any decision regarding their inevitable cohabitation.

She liked - loved him. Tanner owned Thunder Communications. A public relations agency employed by the most famous and infamous to watch out for any negative press and to plug it before it saw print or posted on social media. Carmen knew Tanner when he was on the other side of the business. She always gave him a hard time for those instances he couldn't stop news regarding Ramiro Brandt's idiotic stunts. Most people in the industry would cower at Carmen's fury, but Tanner would fight back. Their head-butting resulted in tokens such as wines or flowers sent in apology. Then they are a casual invitation to some event where they could circulate and make more contacts. Neither knew when exactly meeting for coffee or a meal turned into a date. Still, their business relationship ended the night they fucked in the car parked in Carmen's driveway.

For all her bluster and temper, Carmen was shy, almost timid regarding sex. It took a while for her to become comfortable. She had very few experiences because she was often suspicious of any special attention given to her - and she was right to do so. In high school, the football team had a bet as to who would pop her cherry. A sympathetic classmate alerted her about it. Carmen didn't lose her virginity until she was twenty-four. She had never had romantic prospects but, in the years as manager of Seismic, learned that she could quickly get her next fuck. Carmen still took care, however. She never fucked in her hotel; it was always a guy just passing through. She preferred them a little drunk, so they wouldn't look too closely at her face.

The Seismic members saw her as sexless, or she wasn't their type - not that she ever angled for an affair with any of them - but they respected her. Outside of it, she was feared and dreaded. Tanner Morrison wasn't the least bit intimidated. He looked her right in the eye, snapped back, and didn't hesitate to put her in her place.

He was six feet tall, with lean muscles. His hair was thick, black waves trimmed close to the skull, his round, glinting eyes an exact midnight match. At first, she thought his goatee was stupid, but it grew on her. He liked to surf on the weekends, which explained his perpetual tan. He was more well-groomed than good-looking, clearly, a man who took excellent care of himself and spent a good amount of money on it.

Since the engagement, Carmen and Tanner had been swamped with invitations to various events. She may no longer be the manager of Seismic, but her name still had power. Gone were the days when Carmen babysat five grown men. Now she was a journalist for Rotation, the most prominent music magazine. She interviewed singers and bands and did album reviews. Her articles got the most hits, and every music artist, established or rising, was clamoring to be featured by Carmen.

They had just attended the launch of a new music-sharing site that promised to democratize music distribution yet uphold the artists' rights. Carmen and Tanner hardly had time to enjoy the champagne because everyone wanted to congratulate them or know their take on the new platform. An hour and a half after the launch, Carmen was exhausted and pleaded that they go home.

As she pulled her keys from her purse, Tanner, standing behind her, slid his arms around her waist in a poor pretense of a sweet embrace before his hands dove under her skirt. Her cheeks reddened, her scold breathless and unconvincing as she gripped the key while he mumbled against her shoulder and palmed her pussy. She had to bite back a laugh at the ridiculous image they made. She was red in the face and struggling to remain upright while her fiancé kept his hand on her pussy as if it was going to be stolen from him. Her hands shook as she unlocked the door then they tumbled inside her house. Tanner grunted against her shoulder, fingers fucking her while filling her ear with hot, desperate breathing.

Tanner turned around to claim her lips while stroking and caressing her below the waist. Her dress was a high-necked, black leather number with a zipper from the neckline in front all the way down. The lights were still off, but there was enough light from the moon to see.

A sigh slid from her lips as he found the zipper and tugged it. Carmen smirked as she pushed the dress off while Tanner switched on a lamp. She laughed at his apparent surprise and joy upon discovering she had been naked under her dress all along. He attacked his clothes.

Carmen wailed as Tanner slid his tongue around her nipple, clearly enjoying the added stimulation her piercing gave her. His kisses were wet, hungry slurps on her breasts. They were small but felt heavy with her growing arousal. Tanner tugged a swollen nub too roughly, and she gasped, wordless at how intense the pleasure was.

As Tanner licked and kissed down her flat stomach before pushing his tongue between the drenched folds of her pussy, she groaned and cried out, eyes squeezed shut.

"No fair," she gasped. "I want you too."

"Yeah?" Tanner grinned. "You do?"

"Don't make me beg," she hissed before she used her superior body weight to flip him. Tanner gasped as she climbed over him, turning so she was staring down at his cock.

He spread her thighs wide open as they rested on his shoulders, baring the dripping, pink bounty of her pussy. Carmen whined as she felt his tongue slither into her cunt, his fingers pulling at the skin of her inner thigh to open her wider. Then it was Tanner's turn to grunt as she pumped his cock in her hands and wrapped her lips around the purpled tip. Up and down, she rubbed him with her fingers, and she alternated between hungry, wet licks and open-mouthed kisses on his cock and balls. Her moan caused his cock to harden when he fucked her with his tongue and fingers.

Carmen's body was tight, knowing relief was so close, but Tanner enjoyed torturing her too much. She resolved to make him come first by sucking on his cockhead with all the suction force she could do when she felt a finger entering her rosette.

God, he was such a jerk. He knew she loved it back there. Sometimes, too much.

Her body was seized by the dark pleasure from his fingers. She continued rubbing his cock, though not as vigorously as before. The feeling of his fingers burned, but fuck, it was heaven. Then he was spreading her lips open with his tongue. *Too much.* She couldn't.

She came with a shout, furiously fucking Tanner in the face while her hand picked up the pace. She tried to suck him, but her body was rocking wildly, helpless against the white-hot pleasure surrounding her. Tanner tasted her just as her pussy rippled from orgasm, hitting his tongue with her sweet cum. Carmen refused to do it alone, so with a few more determined strokes and turns, Tanner's cock erupted with a thick stream of semen. He growled.

She managed a smirk before her lips clamped around his cockhead and sucked.

23

. . .

"TURKEY IN THE SPRING," TANNER SAID LATER. HE WAS SITTING UP IN her king-sized bed. Perched on his slender nose was a pair of hipster glasses while scrolling at his tablet. He was shirtless and looked tasty with his rich, golden tan. It was a shame he was wearing jogging pants.

Fresh from a shower, Carmen was patting her hair dry with a towel. Her pale, freckled skin was covered in droplets and nothing else.

"What about Turkey in the spring?" She asked, giving an innocent pop of her hip when Tanner glanced at her and smiled in approval at her naked state.

"Our wedding."

Carmen left her towel at the foot of the bed and went to the dresser for clothes. As she pulled out a t-shirt and a pair of boy shorts, she heard Tanner moving into the bed.

"Turkey is the hottest place on earth but it's really beautiful in the spring. The beaches, the colors . . . "Dressed now, Carmen turned to find Tanner lying on his back at the foot of the bed, eyes on the tablet while speaking. He had pushed her towel aside. "Or we can do a winter wedding in Switzerland."

"Must we make a ceremony out of it?" Carmen asked as she climbed to her side of the bed. Eyes still on the screen, Tanner stroked the leg she stretched toward him. "I was thinking more of city hall, with just immediate family and a few close friends." Tanner still had a family, but Carmen was an orphan. As for friends . . . she will deal with it when she has to.

"I know you're not into looking like a cupcake on the big day and a big reception," Tanner told her, putting the tablet away and pulling her leg, so it rested on his chest. "But my family is traditional. Don't make me look bad," he scolded her playfully. "Rich, successful PR guy scrimping on his wedding?"

Carmen grinned. "I dare you to try stopping that from getting out."

He sat up, and Carmen trailed her foot suggestively down his navel. He trapped her foot in his hands just before her big toe could push at the waistband of his pants.

"That the kind of wedding you want? City hall?"

"Tanner, what matters to me is the man. I don't give a fuck about cakes and fondant shit and all that. You're what I want." She said. "But if your family insists on a church ceremony . . . "

It made her skin crawl, standing before the crowd while they proclaimed they were each other. Carmen was not comfortable with attention like that. She knew how cruel people could be. But she had Tanner and his family to think about.

Tanner grinned and played with her toes. "I like city hall too but a church ceremony, you in a dress. Knowing what's under all those proper layers." He wiggled his eyebrows.

"Do we have to decide now? We've just gotten engaged."

Carmen adjusted her position as Tanner settled between her legs. Resting his chin on her tummy, he said, "No, we don't have to decide right away. But I want to be with you, Carmen." He took her hand and kissed the ring there. "We've been circling around each other for years. We've wasted so much time."

"Not to me," she told him gently. "We had to grow up a bit. You were a gigantic fucktard when we first met."

Tanner chuckled and kissed her navel. "I must have improved to have won the hand of the mighty Carmen."

She played with his curls. "These days, you're just a fuck."

"I'll take it." He rose a bit and pulled at her shorts. "And this."

As Carmen raised her hips to help him shimmy her bottoms down, her phone on the nightstand started to vibrate. She glanced at it as Tanner spread her legs and settled between them.

A name. Ramiro. On and on, and the screen flashed. *Ramiro. Ramiro. Ramiro.*

POISED TO SLAY HER AGAIN, TANNER ASKED, "SOMEONE IMPORTANT?"

Carmen hit IGNORE, and the phone went quiet. She relaxed against the pillows with a sigh. She urged Tanner to lower his head to her cunt, ignoring the heaviness in her heart, the voice screaming at her. His tongue pressed on her clit.

"Not anymore."

CHAPTER 4

Dear Carmen,

You might be surprised to get a letter from me like this. It's been one month since I last tried contacting you. Whatever you think, I am calling not to be bailed out of trouble again but to tell you that I am leaving.

You said things the last time we were together that really hit home. They were things people have been telling me, Robin, especially, but it's you that reached something inside me that made me think. You were there from the early days of Seismic, so you're one of the few people who know me best. The number who believe me as you do - well, that's only you.

After you dropped me off, I couldn't stop thinking. I was angry and disappointed that you wouldn't help me anymore. We were friends. We are friends. I was wallowing in it, so I didn't realize how much I have been hurting you. I guess I'm a hero of sorts in your eyes? If I am, I wish you'd look elsewhere. I'm no one to be looked up to, least admired. I'm more deplorable than you think, and it isn't because of the drugs and alcohol. I don't deserve someone like you.

If you think of replying to my letter, The Retreat isn't one of those centers that aggressively tackle addiction problems. It's a forgiving place. I can come and go as I please. We're assigned little tasks first - mine is cooking and cleaning up the kitchen - before we progress to bigger ones and start getting rewards. Rewards are net access for an hour or a day of doing whatever we want. Things like that. So I'm writing you an old-fashioned letter because all I have now, aside from dishpan hands and the bare necessities, is pen and paper. That's it.

I'll end here. I just thought to write in case you wonder where I went. You're all about tough love, but you have a marshmallow heart for Ramiro. This proves I didn't die choking on my vomit because I passed out drunk. A month may be too soon to say anything, but I'm not as fucked up anymore.

Yours, Ramiro.

SEPTEMBER *30*

Dear Carmen,

Still angry with me? I don't blame you.

Writing you this letter isn't going to help me at all with you, but . . . I'm still doing it. There's something about writing letters that's therapeutic. Is it the soft whisper of the pen across the paper? Is it because I imagine you just across from me as I write this, your ridiculous eyes looking very blue. You do have silly eyes. That's what prompted me to write this. The sea over here shines like sapphires at a particular hour in the day, and I was reminded of you.

That last time you got me, you told me you were engaged? To some guy? Oliver? Something like that? How's that?

Carmen, I said in my previous letter that I wished you'd admire someone else because all your efforts would be wasted on me. I take it back. I can handle my father not thinking so much of me; Robin believes everyone is an idiot. But you - I can't deal with you thinking so little of me. So I hope, as always, you didn't do as I asked.

While cleaning the kitchen, I heard an old Seismic song on the radio. `Battle at Blood.' Do you remember the night it was written? Euan and I are just *fiddling with our guitars. You were on the couch sleeping. It's the fastest song we've ever done. I miss working with Euan. I forget how you looked when we played that song to you. You looked ready to kill us because we woke you up, but you smiled when I started singing. You sat up and hugged your knees. You watched me sing with those eyes.*

I miss the old days.

I miss you.

Yours, Ramiro.

OCTOBER 22

Dear Carmen,

Today was my last with kitchen duties. I've advanced to cleaning the bedrooms on the second floor, and from there, who knows?.

I know you're getting my letters but are you still angry with me? I am sorry, Carmen. Last week, the session's topic was taking accountability for our actions. I blame no one for why I turned to substances. But hurting you - unfortunately, that's all me.

We have group sessions and also individual sessions. The latter is optional, but I want to get to the heart of my problems. The shrink says I'm resistant but who won't be? I'm an asshole, but I do not relish sitting on a couch for an hour telling some stranger things about myself. I'd rather it be you.

How are things? Are you still engaged?

You're not answering me; you still want to drown me, OR you're fucking all over. By God, Carmen, behave yourself.

Yours, Ramiro

To: Carmen@wmail.com

From: Beast_Ramiro@wmail.com

Date: November 1

Subject: Hello

Hey,

So I'm emailing now.

The shrink says that your name comes up quite often in our sessions. Yours and Temperence's. I said it's because you were my manager and I'd like to think, one of the few true friends I have. He asked me to describe our relationship, and for God's love, I can't find the words.

With Temperance, it was easy. She's my sister. It has always been complicated. You know how she is.

You give me hell. I hated that one time you imposed a curfew on me during a tour because I was staying out all night and unable to perform during rehearsals. I hated you when you camped at the door to block my way, and you totally deserved it when I tripped on you. I regret hurting you when I fell, though. I'm sorry you landed in the hospital and broke a rib.

You seem to know me better than I know myself. Better than anyone does, really. When Lennon and I nearly came to blows during our last rehearsals, you put yourself between us before dragging me out for fresh air. I didn't want to hit him. I only wanted him to think that. But you don't wish to anyone bloodying my beautiful face.

You've seen me at my worst. Instead of staying at my side, you left me.

I can understand that.

You showed me what I had to do by leaving.

Please write back.

Yours, Ramiro

Carmen reread Ramiro's email before she closed her laptop.

Tanner was in the shower. She glanced at the bedroom door before pulling at the drawer under her desk. Nestled along with tickets from Seismic's first significant concert were his three letters.

She opened them and reread them, one by one. In all was the voice of a man determined to change his life. That was good. Carmen had gotten fed up with Ramiro's behavior, but she never stopped believing that he would do the right thing. He was on the road to that. But he still had a ways to go.

His letters were unanswered because she didn't know what to say to him. Ramiro said they were friends, but for her, they were business associates, partners with mutual respect rather than friends. They hung out and ribbed at each other but had no intimacies of friendship. She looked after Seismic and helped them out because it was expected of her. She was the manager.

Members of the Seismic had drifted away to do their own thing after disbanding. Carmen ran into them every once in a while, and they would reminisce about the old days. But that was all.

Still, for Ramiro to write to her. Three handwritten letters, no less.

Her cheeks warmed as her mind veered. She refused to acknowledge, would never admit. It was bad enough that Temperance picked up on it and nearly caused the band to end early on. But it was more difficult now, even with her gone. Whatever feelings Carmen may have had towards Ramiro, she could say they were gone now. Passing notion of a much younger heart back in the day. She had a relationship with Tanner Morrison. A romantic, adult relationship, she thought to herself, looking down at her ring.

Carmen and Tanner now lived together. He had the more prominent place, but her house was closer to their work, so for practical purposes, they settled here. She had never lived with anyone before, so they were still at that awkward phase of adjusting to each other - more so with Tanner. He was selling his apartment, and most of his stuff was in storage. Carmen did her best to make him feel comfort-able - at home - but there were many things that just couldn't be done right. Naively, she had only cleared space in the walk-in closet for him and a shelf in the bathroom. She hadn't realized that she would have to make room for another life.

During the first two weeks, whatever awkwardness or wrong happened in the early days of living together had them resolving things by fucking on any flat surface. They soon realized that not everything could be determined by a tit show or a kiss, and they may face bigger problems than they realized.

For one, Tanner kept nagging her to set the date. She used to reason that they had just gotten engaged, but three months had passed since the night. For her, there was no need to rush. They weren't planning on a long engagement but did Tanner think that once engaged, wedding bells followed soon after? They couldn't even pick up their laundry on time.

Another thing she should not complain about was . . . well, the fucking. They were fucking nearly all the time. Carmen worried that Tanner might be a sex addict because he always wanted it. Really, really did. She was OK with one weekend of fucking, but when it got in the way of sleep, when a cock was jammed in her cunt before she could even stretch first thing in the morning, it was too much. Sometimes she arranged to be out during the weekend, picking an assignment that put her in another time zone, if possible.

Tanner had offered her a job in his firm. He wanted her to take it, and she was an idiot not to. The pay was generous, the opportunity immense, and she got to work with her fiancé. Most women would flip at a chance like this but not Carmen. She already lived with him. He was in her often. They were getting married.

Perhaps the worst thing she did was hide Ramiro from Tanner. Tanner knew Ramiro - the three of them had worked together before. Tanner had zero sympathies for Ramiro and wouldn't tolerate anything from him unless it involved money in the six figures. But Carmen and Ramiro knew each other longer, and out of a sense of old loyalty, she felt protective of him. She hated having to hide Ramiro's correspondence from Tanner. For Tanner, she ceased all things Seismic the day they disbanded. He would never understand that the band was her life for twelve years. It was easy to let Lennon, Russell, Lucas, and Euan drift away but not Ramiro.

And she was proud of him for getting to the Retreat to deal with his demons.

Carmen tucked his letters back in the drawer and opened her laptop. Flexed her fingers, she did, then began to type.

Dear Ramiro,

I have been getting your letters. I'm sorry for not answering. I've been . . .

Carmen frowned.

"Busy," she said aloud and typed it. Yeah. The generic safe answer. She couldn't write, "I've been unable to answer because my fiancé won't let me out of bed and even if I was, his dick would always find itself in me."

Dear Ramiro,

I have been getting your letters. I'm sorry for not answering. I've been busy. I'm a music journalist now; isn't that a riot? So I'm often traveling to cover concerts and shows and do interviews.

I'm glad you're doing well. I always knew you'd shape up. I am sorry that I did it the way I did. I hated myself for not answering your last call, especially now that I know your reason. I promise you that the next time you call, I will answer. I haven't been a perfect friend, I'm afraid. I hope you'll give me a chance.

Come back soon.

Love, Carmen

CHAPTER 5

 *ne year later*

As a peace offering, Carmen went to Tarts & Co. for their dark chocolate cream tart, Tanner's favorite. She tapped her fingers on the counter as it was wrapped up, her stomach a tangle of frayed knots.

They had been arguing a lot for months now. The littlest thing blossomed into screaming matches and slammed doors or Tanner spending the night on the couch. Mornings were sullen as they sat on opposite ends of the table and ignored each other. The nights were just as bad because the bed, once crowded, was suddenly the vastest, loneliest space. Carmen tossed and turned to wonder how she could fix them if they were still fixable.

It was hard to pinpoint when it began but warring over floss left at the sink, and the toilet seat left up, were arguments over what they should be screaming at each other about. Carmen envisioned them in a perpetual haze of love and romance when they got engaged. They had that, even during the early days of Tanner's move. The romance was never their problem, but commitment, particularly hers, was becoming questionable, according to him, when they fought this morning.

That set her off and sent them on a screaming rampage. Past the point of hurt was an anger that had Carmen really tempted to physically hurt Tanner because how dare he implies she was cheating. She never had and was never tempted. It was unfair and just plain wrong, and she yelled that if he couldn't trust her, she would never marry him.

ALL DAY HER MOOD SWITCHED FROM ANGER TO REGRET, THEN BACK. Before things got really complicated, she had to ask Tanner to stop nagging her. Couldn't they enjoy being engaged first? Because she did. And he did as asked but only for as long. She counted the days the subject was never brought up - twelve days. Twelve *wonderful* days of freedom from his morning utterances of getting married in River View as he fucked her. And because the world liked to crap on good things, people got married left and right soon after.

They were invited to five weddings that they couldn't skip - or rather, Carmen couldn't. While dancing at the wedding of his brother Dean, Tanner whispered that they could have a themed wedding or a mix of traditions, where she was from, and his culture. She was thankful when the bride suddenly called for the bouquet toss. About a minute before, she found her hands around a bunch of roses, caught due to her height advantage and long limbs. She had to give Tanner a blow job in the car to shut him up about weddings.

The next was the wedding of Lennon to Caitlin Gunn, her best friend. Carmen was a bridesmaid, and Tanner filled her ears with whispers of how she would walk on a carpet of flowers instead of a mere path like Caitlin did when it was her turn to be the bride. Carmen stood by the champagne fountain the entire night and was unusually friendly, forcing Tanner to circulate on his own. Tanner didn't mention one word regarding weddings for three whole days - the time she had to recover from the hangover.

The next weddings were business associates of Tanner's. Being mere guests had Tanner comparing the decorations to their projected wedding more bluntly, and he just wouldn't let up. After the fifth wedding, Carmen reached her breaking point and told Tanner that if he wasn't going to let her think about the wedding on her own, there would never be a wedding for them. He told her she was shit and wasn't taking their relationship seriously.

She took it back. She knew how the discord in their relationship began. That day. When she said her piece and Tanner accused her of not taking their relationship seriously. It was hurtful because the exact opposite was true. He couldn't fathom that she couldn't think when barraged and nagged left and right about getting hitched. And with Tanner now living with her, there was hardly any room to breathe.

Carmen threw herself to work for the whole day. She turned in two articles in advance, saw someone who tried to convince her to venture into producing music, and then producers for a new reality show looking to form the next big rock band. They wanted her as one of the mentors.

Tanner's low-slung Black Thunder was already parked when she swung the car towards their house. She parked behind him, leaving enough space for when he left early in the morning. She took the gleaming silver paper bag of Tarts & Co. and walked up to the front door.

"I'm home," she called out, closing the door behind her and walking inside. The silver bag was placed on the kitchen counter before her feet brought her to the bedroom. A blond eyebrow cocked at the sight of an open suitcase at the foot of the bed. The door from the closet swung open, and Tanner, a few clothes in his arms, gave her a startled look.

They stared at each other, Carmen's questioning and him stoic. Then he looked away and brushed past her shoulder as he put his clothes in the bag. Wordlessly, her eyes followed him as he took a few underwears from the dresser.

"I know things have not been good for a while but this isn't the answer, Tanner," she managed to say.

"Relax. I'll be away for a couple of days, that's all," he muttered, dumping his underwear in the bag. He still wouldn't look at her.

"Where are you going?" Carmen asked a moment later when he offered no further information. Instead, he was looking at his phone. She hated that her voice sounded as small as a child's.

"Tina Hanson was busted for possession at the airport. Her agent and I will be doing damage control for a few days." He answered, sounding like his teeth were being pulled one by one.

"Oh." Tina was a young actress, gorgeous but a mess. Tanner zipped up his bag.

"There's dark chocolate tart from Tart Co's," Carmen said as another yawning silence fell between them. Tanner tossed his phone on the bed and stomped to their closet, wrenching off his suit with sharp, jerking motions. Her mouth usually went dry at the sight of his glorious, tanned skin and muscles, but her throat was tight from a fear she couldn't voice out. "I - I am sorry for this morning, Tanner. I really am."

"We should use the time apart to think," was his answer, putting on a crisp, black shirt. Then he put on the suit jacket he had discarded and strolled out of the closet. His dark eyes rested briefly on her before he took his suitcase and walked out of the room.

"I don't need to think," Carmen yelled as she went after him. Being taller and with longer legs, she quickly overtook him and planted her body right between him and the door. "Tanner, I love you. Please don't doubt that."

His eyes were cold as they stared back at her. She flinched as if struck.

"Then tell me you'll marry me."

"I am."

"When." His voice was gruff. He was still angry. "Tell me when."

"I can't - "she started to say, and he rolled his eyes, going around her to head for the door. Helplessly, she watched as he reached the door. "Tanner, it's not like that. We have to decide on that together."

"I think I've made it clear that where or when or how doesn't matter, just as long as I marry you," he said, putting the suitcase down and turning to her. "You're the one dragging her feet."

"I'll marry you now if you want," she declared.

Tanner shook his head. "Is that what *you* want?"

When she didn't answer immediately, he sighed and picked up the bag. "I thought so."

"Tanner - "

"I'll see you when I return, Carmen. The service is here."

Then he was gone.

Carmen hugged herself, shaking violently as the house's silence assaulted her. No tears came, but a choking sensation spread in her throat, her eyes dry and sandy. Goosebumps rose as her skin damp-ened. Closing her eyes, her arms dropped to the sides. She plunked hard on the sofa and put her head between her legs.

Her erratic breathing eventually slowed. She raised her head and slid on her butt toward the floor. I love you, but I need more time, she should have told Tanner, except she knew he wasn't going to give it to her. She was a fool for wanting more time to be not Mrs. Tanner Morrison. He loved and desired her, and he was hurt by her apparent rejection and lack of commitment. She didn't know why the idea of finally marrying him left her cold and scared. Her feelings for him were true, but something in her, from somewhere, told her to wait. For what, she didn't know.

In times like this, she would go to her desk and get Ramiro's hand-written letters. They emailed for about a month before she asked if he would mind writing her the old-fashioned way. His handwriting gave her headaches, and the things he wrote both annoyed and amused her. They exchanged letters, and it was on the paper she wrote on that she to be at her most honest.

She chided him for not remembering Tanner ("He's the guy that stopped that paparazzi from selling the photo of you throwing up in front of Onyx Club") and told him she was proud of him and believed in him.

He was a friend, but she only realized it recently. It made her a total dunce, really. They didn't share their deepest, darkest secrets, but talking was always easy. At least, until Temperance would call Ramiro on his cell and demand that he come to her, or when she went on tour with them, rap on Carmen's door and tell Ramiro he had to leave. She always knew when to time her arrival - just when either Ramiro or Carmen was on the verge of sharing something important, put into words after a long time. Ramiro clearly didn't want to go, but he kissed Carmen on the cheek in apology and did as his sister demanded.

Carmen couldn't figure out their relationship, and when she asked the guys, they said they were always close. Their mother died, and Temperance had grown totally dependent on Ramiro. They thought she was a drag and had told Ramiro to man up about her, but it was pointless. He was devoted to his sister. Carmen didn't think to ask Ramiro himself. The dagger looks Temperance gave her were more than enough warning.

When Ramiro left, Carmen left the room too. Her destination would be a bar that was far enough that she won't be tempted to bring the guy back to her room, yet it wasn't that big of a hassle to drive back to. An emptiness hit her

hard when Ramiro left, and it left her restless. A stranger's cock made her forget the soreness in her cunt, the drug that put her to sleep upon her return.

Carmen took the box of letters and brought them to the kitchen with her. She hated food to go to waste, so she helped herself to a piece of the tart and popped open a bottle of her favorite brandy. Then she took the food, the bottle, and the box to the couch.

She could imagine Ramiro looking exasperated when he wrote, his green eyes twinkling with amusement as he fired off word after word. People would say they had a romance, but it wasn't. It was friendship. Carmen was glad that Ramiro was making the time to work out whatever issues were plaguing him. While she hoped he would sing again and command the stage, she never told him. Ramiro mentioned he missed the creative process behind a song, the writing, the composing, and the collaboration. He asked her once if she was in touch with former Seismic members, and she mentioned Lennon's wedding. But she added she didn't see much of them anymore. She kept tabs, though.

They had all gone into music production and had unique collaborations with other artists and groups. Carmen asked Euan why they didn't continue with the band with another singer. He told her that though Ramiro was a gigantic asshole, it felt wrong and disloyal to work with each other without him. Ramiro was the one to put the band together, so the guys would always be thankful to him.

Ramiro's last letter was from a month ago. They wrote a lot but only sometimes. Sometimes months would pass before another note came along. She read this lying on the couch. It was her favorite because he sounded like the old Ramiro again, snarky dashed with self-assured arrogance, amused and mocking.

Done, she put it in the box and kept print-outs of his emails. The heaviness and tension in her body had eased, but she could still be a little more relaxed. She put away her plate and the wine and went to the bedroom.

Her favorite thing in her house was not the bedroom but the hot tub. This was her indulgence, soaking in the warm bubbles and the jets underneath pounding and hitting her muscles. It was best accessed through her bedroom to ensure privacy, but one could also walk around the property to get there. With the high walls surrounding the house, Carmen didn't worry about being watched - not that there was much to see. The cluster of lemon trees in the garden surrounding the house provided more cover.

She filled it with water and then changed into an old, faded blue bikini. The halter style lifted her tiny tits toward each other, so in a particular light, she had what looked to be cleavage. Her broad shoulders didn't look mannish, although teeny bits of fabric bared her muscular physique. The bottom was the low, hip-skimming style. Her bush was full and thick as she hadn't gone to the waxer for two months. She tucked the hair into the panel of the bikini and then realized it was ridiculous. She was home alone, and it was her hot tub. On her way out, she grabbed a towel and put her phone in a dock. She swiped the screen until she found her Seismic playlist, then put it on random play. She turned the volume up and left the door from her room to the bath open to hearing the music.

She turned on the tub and fixed the settings. It was a fantastic night out, but she was content to wait for a few minutes before dipping a toe into the bubbly water and then the rest of her. "God," she groaned as excellent, hot water embraced her. She momentarily dunked her head in the water and then laughed. Her body slid across the tub to lean against the edge. With a contented sigh, she closed her eyes.

Heaven on earth. She had a hot tub, listening to music from her favorite band. In her house with the mortgage paid for. The two glasses of wine she'd had made her body delightfully slugging. A stream of shaky groans stuttered out of her lips as the jets and sprays pounded on her spine, the back of her shoulders, all the way down. In her relaxed state, her legs fell wide open.

A column of water rushed right toward her, right between her legs.

Her eyes flew open. "Oh, God. *Fuck.*"

Flames licked her cheeks as she began to move away, then thought, why not?

Fighting with Tanner meant they were excellent in bed or slept apart. Carmen estimated that at least a month had passed since they last fucked. Out of loyalty to him and embarrassment, she had thrown out her favorite battery-operated devices. Her eyebrows furrowed as she stared at the bubbling water around her, the pressure of the jets underneath tempting like a caress. Self-consciously, she glanced around.

She spread her legs and grunted as the water hit her right *there.*

"God."

SPREADING HER ARMS ON THE TUB'S EDGE, SHE SUBMITTED TO THE FORCE of the water. Her long legs floated up as what felt like a thousand heavy tongues teased her inner thighs and aching center. The sensation seemed to rise and wrap around her waist, making her giggle as it tickled her. The sound of her joy suddenly stopped when she felt a hard jet of water brush against her tits. It didn't take long for her nipples to tighten painfully. Eyes screwed shut, she attacked the ties of her top and then threw it away unseen. Her spine arched at the delicious sensations overwhelming every inch of her body, *all* the orifices. Wow, that felt *insanely* good back there.

"Oh, god."

Hissing, she reached under the water and yanked at her bottoms. As the licking sensation continued, her finger joined in the effort. A rough mewl was torn from her lips when she felt how hard and fat her clitoris was. God, how was that even possible? She couldn't remember her clit being this brutal, her cunt aching and swelling so much, and Tanner was a fantastic lover. She pressed her finger on her clit, and rotated it. Her eyes flew open as she cried out, shakes seizing her body.

She collapsed against the edge of the tub, fucking herself furiously. Her other hand cupped her tit and began to squeeze and pinch a tight nipple. As she groaned and hissed, the iPod shuffled to Seismic's most famous song, The Lady Is A Minx. It was a fast, drum-heavy song with insane guitar riffs. Ramiro's voice was a sexy growl as he sang about stiff-collared librarians that were hot as sin underneath. Through the haze of her lust, she heard him singing about blond minxes with angel eyes. Her mind latched to those words," *Blond minxes, angel eyes, blond minxes, angel eyes . . .* "

Her breathing sped up as if she were running. She was flushed and pink as she chased the orgasm the water jets cruelly dangled before like an elusive treat. Her fingers' sensual rubbing and pinching harshened, and she shrieked, feeling suddenly flung and flying. On and on, she continued touching herself, hips moving against the insane water jets. At the very peak of her release, her eyes flew open, and she saw orbs of gold and green. Blondes and angel eyes.

"Angel eyes," she whispered before slumping back in the tub, her eyes closing again. Her arms and legs fell limp on their sides, and she would have gone under if she didn't reach for the edge of the tub. Sighing and humming, her body felt soft and buoyant after her orgasm. A sleepy, satisfied smile spread across her lips, and she looked up at the night sky. Black and splashed with stars. What a perfect end to a perfect bath.

Her eyes started to drift close again when the unmistakable, rough sound of a *human* clearing his throat hit her. Horrified that someone had seen, she opened her eyes and shot to her feet, ready to attack the intruder. Gold and green spots continued to dance before her, and she had to shake her head to clear her vision and see -

"What the hell are you doing in my yard, Ramiro Brandt?"

Eyes the color of fire made a slow caress from the top of her pink forehead to the wet, dripping dark blond muff between her thighs.

The dimples surrounding the most arrogant smirk on the planet deepened.

"Fuck, Carmen, but that body is a sight for sore eyes."

Realizing she was fucking butt-naked, Carmen fell back on the tub and hit her head.

For once, the fates were kind enough to knock her out.

CHAPTER 6

Ramiro only had a moment to grimace at Carmen's head banging on the concrete tub before he sprang into action. Shoes, pants, and all, he leaped into the water and caught her just as she went under. The warm caress of the water and the slick skin of the beautiful woman in his arms only contributed to his pants' twitching problem. Difficult to ignore because of the pain, but it couldn't overwhelm his worry at Carmen limp and unconscious. She was stern and surprisingly very heavy since she looked lean, bordering on skinny. His legs suddenly gave way, and with a startled shout, they both fell into the water. One of his arms flung to the side, palm slapping hard on the tub's frame while he kept the other around her waist. She started to slip into his arms, and he grabbed hold of her again, realizing immediately that he was cupping her left tit. Carmen moaned and began to stir.

"Shit," he muttered, dumbly staring at his hand still on her tit, feeling the soft skin and something cool and unyielding around her nipples. Annoyed with himself, he lowered his hand to her waist, tightened it, and drew them to the edge of the tub where he could lean and keep them afloat.

"Carmen?" His other hand gently slapped her pink cheek. "Sweetheart?"

Her eyes remained closed. He noticed that her eyelashes were blond and thin but curled almost delicately. Her lips moved, so he put his ear close to them. As he did, something glinted below her neck. "What - What?" He pressed her, eyes riveted at the gleaming silver studs framing her pink nipple and the delicate filigreed design of what appeared to be the shape of stars around her big aureoles. He had to swallow a tortured-sounding grunt as the pressure between his thighs increased.

"Whatcha doin' here," she slurred. Worried even more, he tore his eyes away from the exciting and surprising jewelry set she was wearing and turned to look at her. Her eyes were the color of midnight blue under the overhead lights as they stared at him.

"Hey," he greeted her, pushing a wet tendril of her hair from her forehead.

She sighed then her eyes fell closed. Panicking, he shook her awake. "No, no, no. Carmen, you can't sleep, alright? I'm taking you to the hospital to get your head checked." As her eyes blinked open, her forehead scrunched as if in deep thought.

"I'm okay," she muttered, but her stare was a little unfocused.

"Let's see what the doctor has to say about that," Ramiro growled as he planted his feet firmly on the slippery floor of the tub and rose, carrying her now. She was squirming and murmuring nonsense about being heavy and delicate, so he told her to shut it. He thought it was stupid of her to cover her tits and told her so. She grunted something about castrating him as soon as she had the chance.

Puddles of watermarked their route, Ramiro deducing the open door near the tub must mean it was either the bathroom or something with clothes. A bedroom, it turned out. His wet pants flapped, and his shoes squished at every step until he sat her in bed. Carmen was still staring dully at him, and he gently felt her head for a bump. When he found the rise along her skull, she gasped, "Ow! What the fuck, Ramiro!" She exclaimed, her voice clear and outraged.

"There's the Carmen I know and love," he shot back, retracting his fingers. As she grunted that she needed clothes, he found a soft gray throw left on a chair and draped it on her shoulders. It covered her just about, from the neck down to her hips, and she had to keep her legs together, but Ramiro had already seen the cunt she was guarding. No way was he forgetting that.

"Where are your clothes?" He demanded, looking around the room.

"I can get dressed myself," Carmen insisted stubbornly, her hand tenderly touching the spot on her head that throbbed.

"Sure, if you want to give me another show," he told her, crossing his arms and staring down at her. She turned red and huddled under the little throw.

He almost wished she would because he had *no idea* she was hiding a body like that under all her good sweaters and boring dark suits. He knew she didn't wear bras since her nipples were always hard around him. Still, when you worked in a business where every other woman flashed her goodies at you, you got unaffected by all that. But it had been more than a year. Carmen's body did not have the soft contours expected of a woman. Still, he hadn't fucked for so long that it was no wonder his cock stirred at her sweet-looking little tits, boyish waist, and hairy cunt. The overlong dry spell he had cruelly subjected his body to make him more intrigued than he should be about what those wet hairs were hiding.

"Clothes, Carmen," he told her again. "Unless you want me to take you to the hospital like that."

She glared at him. "I don't need to go to the hospital."

"Tell me that again by looking at me right in the eye. You can't even focus. I'd bet you're seeing two of me. Lucky you." He said. Again, he demanded, "Your clothes or we leave with you like that." He crossed his arms and gave her a look that said it was no bluff.

47

Scowling, she wearily pointed at the door behind him.

Ramiro opened the closet and identified her side there. The other side boasted a long rack of tailored suits in varying shades of steel, gray, and charcoal. He took a familiar-looking blue sweater and a pair of jeans. He opened several drawers to find scarves, watches, and some jewelry but no underwear.

His cock got impossibly hard at the idea that Carmen probably didn't wear panties.

Fuck, Brandt. Stop behaving like you're the one who got hit. He went to the other side of the closet and found a pair of jogging pants and a t-shirt. The pants were a bit snug and ended right above his ankles, but they were dry, at least. He skipped underwear, too, though he was still clearly erect. Tanner's shoes were too small, so he went to Carmen's side of the closet and helped himself to her running shoes. They fit perfectly. Dressed, he walked out of the closet.

She muttered some thanks - or at least, that's what it sounded when he handed her the clothes. "Turn around," she said.

Ramiro had to smirk. "Carmen, sweetheart, I've already seen every-thing and more. I think it's pointless to be shy."

"Fuck you."

Despite what he said, he busied himself with touching and fiddling with random objects in the room. It wasn't really his fault that there was a mirror there angled such that he saw her nude again. God above, he hadn't pegged his former manager as the sort to have nipple piercings, let alone go commando. It didn't escape his notice of the absence of her complaint regarding the underwear. His eyes burned at the sight of the aperture that divided the firm, high cheeks of her ass at the bulging muscles of her thighs. Ramiro didn't believe in god, but he was praying to be put out of his misery as he gazed longingly at the irresistible sway of her hips before she *bent* to put on the jeans. *Some-body kill me now.* One of God must have heard him because, mercifully, the denim covered those freckles and pale skin. He turned around and watched her zipping up.

Standing taller than him, pink-cheeked, and looking sleepy, she reiterated about not needing to go to the hospital.

Stubborn mule." For my own peace of mind, let's go have it checked. Besides, I need the doctor's go-ahead before I talk to you about something important," he said, and she was back to muttering under her breath again. "Remember what happened before, when I fell on you because you had that idiotic plan of literally blocking my way from having a good time? You were whimpering like a motherless puppy clutching your side and if I hadn't insisted on bringing you to the hospital we wouldn't have known about your broken rib."

She glared at him when he moved to carry her again, so he sighed loudly and dropped his arms. She grabbed her purse and trailed after him as they left the bedroom. He had been to her house before, just never in the bedroom and certainly not the hot tub area. But he knew that she kept a bowl by the door which housed the keys. They were scooped and secured in his hand before she could protest.

He drove to Mother Mercy General Hospital. Again, Carmen refused his assistance, but he ignored her this time and yanked her behind him by the hand. Their wait in the emergency room wasn't very long due to her head injury.

Ramiro refused to leave Carmen while waiting for the doctor in the exam room. Her speech was clear now, and her eyes focused when glaring at him, but he wanted her head scanned and examined. Sensing that Carmen would like their visit to be over quick, Ramiro was determined to stay with her to ensure that her examination was thorough.

Waiting still, Carmen finally asked Ramiro the question that had been nagging her since finding him in her yard.

"When did you leave home? You didn't mention it in your last letter."

"That's because I had no intention of leaving at the time."

Frowning, she asked, "What happened?"

He pinched the bridge of his elegant nose. "Carmen, let's talk about it after you're examined, alright?"

"I'm fine," she insisted stubbornly. "I'm not seeing double."

"You're way cranky than usual. It might be a symptom," he said, sitting beside her on the bed.

"Ramiro, every time you're in a room, you annoy the hell out of people. Even without speaking."

He smiled. "You mean I don't have to do anything and I already affect people so profoundly?"

"God, Ramiro. How is it that your head isn't any bigger?"

He shrugged and glanced at her left hand. "I see the ring's still on. Tanner Morrison, ringtone, complained to the band once that the guy they hired to do the PR had a cunt name. Who the hell names their kid Tanner?

Carmen smirked and snorted. "I can't believe you don't remember him."

"I can't believe he's the guy behind that. He's short and quite oily. You know. Too slick." Ramiro made a face. He remembered Tanner Morrison as a too-slick guy who wore a lot of blacks and one he didn't really trust. The guy must be hung for someone like Carmen to be gaga over him. Engaged, no less. "He reeks like a car salesman."

"He does not! Tanner smells like lemons and he smells great."

He cocked an eyebrow. "I don't really trust that. You just hit your head."

"Another crack like that and you'll end up the same way."

How could he have gone more than a year without riling her up? "So I suppose I'll have to ask you another time if you always get off listening to my songs, huh?"

Her face went from pale to fire-engine red in three seconds. "For-For the love of god, Ramiro!" She sputtered. Angrily, she slapped his placating hands and jumped off the bed. He grabbed her by the waist and hauled her back to his chest. She struggled, but he was stronger despite sitting down. He grunted as he slightly twisted his lower body away from her hip. His cock had begun to behave, but with her squirming and brushing against him, it was raring to go.

"Let me go," she hissed.

"Cool it, will you? Can't you take some teasing . . . "He smirked against her hair. "Minx?"

"Damn it, Ramiro!"

"Alright. I'll shut up now. I'll wait until you're in your fighting form before I ask again. Minx." He was practically purring. He didn't know water had a scent, but that was what he smelled from behind her ear. Fresh and natural. Carmen jerked away from him and sat back down.

The curtain parted, and a tall man with the wildest red hair and a frightful-looking beard entered. Ramiro's arm flung protectively across Carmen's chest before he saw the white coat he was wearing, and the stethoscope slung across his shoulders. The man looked like a half-bear and half-man.

"Which one of you is Carmen Schwartz?"

Ramiro lowered his hand to her knee and patted it soundly. "Her."

The man frowned at him and then smiled at Carmen. He was practically leering. Ramiro saw Carmen's nipples pointed and strained under her sweater and the fucking bear-man clearly appreciated the sight. When the man introduced himself, Ramiro thought of throwing his t-shirt over her and wrapping her up with the sheet like a burrito. "I'm Dr. McCoy."

"I don't need to be here," Carmen declared.

Ramiro rolled his eyes, moving his arm around her shoulders. "She slipped in the hot tub and hit her head. She was unconscious for a few seconds."

As if remembering that Ramiro was there, the bear-man frowned at him. "What happened?"

Carmen blushed, and Ramiro was quick. Casually, he drawled, "Well, doctor, I don't think my fiancée would like for anyone else to know the precise details of her slipping, but we both had a great time before that." He chuckled. "My sweetheart sure knows how to welcome her man home."

Big, sapphire eyes stared at Ramiro in horror, and he grinned. McCoy's frown deepened as he made a note on the chart and fished out a penlight from his pocket.

"Carmen, let's have a look at you, shall we? You were right to come here if you were unconscious even for just a few seconds."

"Told you," Ramiro said.

"I still think this is a waste of time," Carmen complained, following McCoy's instructions to look at the light. Ramiro tightened his hold on her shoulders when the doctor started feeling for the spot on her head. Carmen's hiss of pain told him he'd found it, and he made another note on the chart.

"Your pupils are responding to the light. How are you feeling?'

Blinking rapidly and squinting, Carmen was cross. "My head hurts and I'm a little sleepy."

"Best that you keep awake for a few hours," he said, writing on the chart again. "Do you have blurred vision? Difficulty speaking?"

"She was slurring when she regained consciousness," Ramiro said.

"But not anymore," Carmen added quickly. "I'm fine."

"Still, to be on the safe side." McCoy wrote some more. When he looked at Ramiro, he was frowning again. "She needs to be kept awake for four hours. She can take the medicine during that time. When she sleeps, she must be awakened every two hours after. Think you can do that?"

"There's no need for that. I can set the alarm," Carmen protested. McCoy looked like he was considering - hell, he preferred this option. Ramiro saw him seem at war with himself before he said with a sigh, "You might sleep through the alarm, Carmen. Best that someone is really there to make sure." He glanced at Ramiro again, this time looking resigned.

Again, Ramiro grinned from ear to ear. "Signing on, doc."

"Are we done?" Carmen was impatient. She gave Ramiro a side-eye. "I told you this is a waste of time."

"Let me write up the prescription for you, then you can go." McCoy told them, then left.

"We saw a doc, so we know what to watch out for," Ramiro said, leaning back on the bed and putting his hands behind him. "You wouldn't want to be the first Schwartz to drown in the bath. Although that could have been a way to go." He waggled his eyebrows suggestively, and Carmen looked away. Her neck was flushed cherry-red.

Enjoying what he was doing, he continued, "I'm surprised you picked *The Lady is A Minx*. I pegged you more as more of *The Fury* sort." The Fury was literally Seismic's loudest song. All shouting and screaming guitar riffs. If Carmen was into complex rock music when fucking, The Fury was just the song for her. Now that was a thought. Buttoned-up, braless Carmen with the nipple piercings must enjoy rock-star-style-screaming sex.

"Would you stop," she hissed.

"Where the fuck is Tanner? Hell, Carmen, if that's the show I'll be coming home to every night I don't think I'll leave at all."

"Ramiro, I swear if you don't shut up - "

Knowing he had pushed her far enough, he held up his hands in surrender. Carmen was still scowling at him when the bear doctor returned. He smiled at Carmen when he handed her paper but gave Ramiro a warning look. The hairy dog was obviously into Carmen. Fat chance he was going further than that.

"Take this when you get home but stay awake for four hours." He told her, his manner very friendly. To Ramiro, he practically snarled, "Then you wake her up every two hours."

As Carmen tucked the prescription in her pocket, Ramiro swept the curtain aside gallantly and gestured she precede him. She ducked her head as she walked past. Without warning, Ramiro slapped her on the ass.

"What on earth - "Carmen growled, whirling around. Ramiro laughed and slapped her there again.

"Still in fine form, minx. Just checking." He smirked at McCoy, who was glaring at him disapprovingly. Carmen grunted under her breath and walked away fast. Ramiro was quickly at her heels, his arms wrapping around her waist. When he looked back, the doctor was staring wistfully after them.

"I knew it," he said, leading Carmen to the pharmacy.

"Get your hands off me," she commanded.

"After I just protected you from that lecher?" Ramiro put his hands on his hips and stared up at her. She wasn't much taller than him, but he still had to crane his neck. He glanced pointedly at her erect nipples. "He really liked you." He said huskily.

Carmen gasped, and her arms quickly flew up to cover her chest. Reddening, she hunched low. Realizing he had embarrassed her, he promptly said, "Hey, it's not your fault. You have every right to not wear a bra. Your tits don't need them - "

"Ramiro, for the love of God, I am this close," she showed the small distance between her thumb and forefinger, "to knocking myself out just so you'll stop torturing me."

He bit back a grin. "I just thought to protect you, minx. That doctor was looking at you like you're a giant lollipop he would like to lick and slurp."

Carmen shot him a withering glare, then turned to make her order to the pharmacist. As her prescription was packed, she turned to Ramiro. Rubbing her eyes, she asked, "Ramiro, you haven't answered my question. Why are you here?"

Deliberately misunderstanding her, he said, "You couldn't believe how handsome I am so you fainted."

She glowered at him, which conveyed she would hack off his body parts with the bluntest blade she could find for added torture. Shifting his weight from one foot to the other, he cleared his throat.

Carmen tapped her foot impatiently. "Out with it."

"I wish to sing again." He looked her in the eye, his voice grave. "I intend to make a comeback, and I need you to make it happen."

CHAPTER 7

As he had been doing since he nearly gave her a heart attack hours ago, Ramiro strolled ahead of her, unlocked her front door, and slipped inside. Carmen limped after him, eyebrows drawn together and thick bottom lip jutting out in a moody pout. She closed the door, tossed her purse on the table, and watched in disbelief as Ramiro went to the kitchen and helped himself to the dark chocolate tart.

Her head was no longer throbbing as it had, but a new headache was about to happen. She continued with her appalled stare as Ramiro rooted in the fridge next and pulled out a carton of milk. He sniffed it, shrugged, and brought it to the table.

"Excuse me?" She demanded. "What the fuck are you doing?"

"I'm starving. Come over here." Ramiro pulled out a chair for her and helped himself to the food.

She must still have been knocked out and drowned in the bathtub. That must be it. She was dead, and this was the first hell in her descent. She went to the kitchen but only stayed by the doorway, her mouth pursed even tighter as Ramiro let out a really indecent, sinfully sexy moan as he bit into the tart. Her eyes widened as she felt a familiar swelling below her stomach.

"God, *fuck*," he spoke, eyes closed as he savored the bite. He licked his lips, and her breath froze halfway before she remembered how to exhale. He closed his eyes and brought his fingers to his lips. Yep. This was hell, alright. No one with greasy, blond hobo hair should look that good eating tart. If Ramiro were cast in a commercial for pastry, everyone would not only forget about the ten pounds they wanted to lose, there would be converts among hard-core vegans and anti-gluten groups too. She was neither.

"Oh, god." Ramiro continued to groan. His voice was doing fluttery things to her stomach and between her thighs. Carmen wanted to kick something. Her head may not be hurting as much anymore, but she was still in a fight with her fiancé, which meant more than a month of not getting any action. She thought herself a decent person, not the kindest nor the nicest. This torture Ramiro was inflicting on her was really, really unfair.

"I'm sorry. I thought we were going to have a serious talk about the impossible task you've set for me." She crossed her arms and gave him a look.

"We can talk while I eat," he said, smacking his lips and opening his eyes. A squinty, emerald stare was aimed at her before he forked another piece off the tart. Either he was oblivious to her annoyance or didn't care. She went for the latter. He gave her a chiding look when she remained by the doorway and said, "Minx, I've been eating non-dairy, organic and vegan shit for a year. How I survived can be told another time but I really am starving."

He reached for the carton of milk, about to glug it down. Carmen hissed and quickly dived for a glass. She set it next to him, eyes narrowed, then sat down heavily. He smiled and poured milk into the glass.

"Don't be an animal. And quit calling me Minx," she said, dropping heavily on the chair next to him.

"Why? It suits you." He winked at her and sipped the milk.

She noticed for the first time that his wrists were bonier than lean, firm muscle. When she first saw him watching her orgasm as he leaned against the tree, she had to look at his eyes to recognize him. The long hair made his face look narrow, his cheekbones sharp thrusts under the skin, and his beard, trimmed neatly, almost made him look . . . well, delicate. Ramiro had always been slim but muscular. Now he was wiry. He looked to have lost around twenty pounds.

Seeing her eyes on his thin wrist, he shrugged. "A year without anything processed - basically not eating anything really good, that's all. And hard labor."

"I hardly call cleaning kitchens labor."

"Oh, no. I was in charge of the stables. Taking care of the horses, feeding them, cleaning the stalls, the like. It's a heavy workload and I'm usually too tired to eat."

"But you were at the retreat to take good care of yourself. You were there to get better, you said."

"I did. I am. But who knows how I am in the real world," he finished the first piece of the tart and helped himself to another. "That's why I had the cab bring me here. I figured you won't have anything to tempt me. However," and this time, his eyes fell on her tits. To her eternal mortification, her nipples tightened painfully and seemed to point toward him. He grinned at her irritation and laughed when she jerked her arms around herself. "I think you just proved me wrong. Nipple piercings and no underwear. You're straight out of my teenage wet dreams, Minx."

"Ramiro, I swear if you don't start getting serious - "she began to snap, her ears burning. Straight out of his wet dreams, indeed! She thought that was one of the many things the retreat failed to fix. Ramiro was more mocking.

He sighed loudly and dug into the tart. "I am serious. I really want to sing again." He said, putting a hand on her wrist to stop her from moving away. His green eyes bored deep into hers, his gaze clear.

Ramiro is singing again. She would die first before admitting she missed hearing him on the radio, that she missed hearing anything new from him even more.

Ramiro was one of the best rock singers and a total performer. He knew how to work for the crowd and would sometimes throw himself into ensuring Seismic performances were talked about for days, even years. Carmen remembered one show where Ramiro, to the shock of the crowd and everyone else in the band, Ramiro strapped on what looked to be a special suit, pressed some controls, and rose from the stage. He sang three songs, circling the crowd from the air. Only Carmen knew about it and thought it was fantastic. The band members didn't think so due to the risk Ramiro took, but he brushed them aside. You had to be reckless to pull off the things he did onstage and off it.

"Singing is my reason for everything, Carmen. It's how I found my voice. My self." Ramiro drained the milk from his glass and refilled it. "I haven't done it for over a year. That's the longest I've been without singing and music. You have no idea how painful it was to give it up to get better."

"You didn't have to." Carmen told him. "Nobody told you to quit."

"It seemed the right thing to do at a time." Ramiro said quietly. As she shook her head, he nodded. "Yes, it was, Carmen. I was only singing because I had to. I forgot that I'm good at it because I loved it. I forgot all about that. Didn't think it was worthwhile after . . . "

Carmen thought he paused to eat again. Instead, he stared off into space. She realized that his hand still rested on her, elegant and graceful with long, slim fingers on her freckly, pale skin. Carefully moving her hand from under it, he suddenly pressed firmly.

"You never asked what started it all."

Carmen stared helplessly as his fingers slid between the tiny arcs of her own. His palm was rough and calloused, but his hand was still beautiful, much more attractive than hers with their short stubby nails. She knew what he was talking about: Temperance.

"Ramiro, I never asked because I don't like to pry."

He loved his sister. It was probably the kind of love she shouldn't think about, but he was destroyed by her death. She didn't just have a front seat during that time. She was right there, devastated and helpless, as Temperence's death slowly chipped away the life from Ramiro Brandt's eyes.

"You know, you're probably the only manager who believes in the proper distance and all that shit," Ramiro dropped her hand, and she put it on her lap. "Your mouth should be washed with soap, and as of tonight, I won't be too far off in saying that you must be a wildcat in bed. But you're. . . exceedingly, annoyingly polite."

She started to flare up when he brought up her apparent sexual behavior, but it was his rough tone at her politeness that got to her. He said it as if disgusted.

Ramiro's eyes were calm. "You have no compunction telling record execs to fuck themselves raw; you relish killing them during contract negotiations. Doubtless, there's hardly a thing you wouldn't do for Seismic. Oh, I know. You refuse to have any relationship past the professional with us. We're not friends."

"I don't know what you're talking about. Are you done?" Without waiting for his answer, she took his used plate, fork, and glass and brought them to the sink.

"We've known each other for almost fifteen years, minx." Ramiro continued speaking from behind her as she started washing. "You know I'm allergic to strawberries, that Euan sometimes sleepwalks, Lennon is not on good terms with his family. You know that Lucas can't be given painkillers because he got addicted to them before. But we - I - know nothing about you except that you would probably kill for us, won't you?"

"Don't flatter yourself. I'm just a dedicated employee."

"You started out like that but you have to believe me when I say I think of you as a friend. Outside of the band, you're the only other real friend I have." Ramiro's laugh was bitter. "The only one I have left, come to think of it."

Carmen finished washing them and then put them on the rack to dry. Wiping her hands, she turned around to look at Ramiro. He was still sitting down, arms folded on the table and looking at her in puzzlement and frustration.

"We can't be friends if you want me to remain good at my job, Ramiro. And admit it: I am the fucking best."

"You are. But I'm curious if you've ever cared about any of us.

"Of course I did. I made the arrangements for Temperence's funeral. I kept the press away - "

"Drove me to morgue and allowed me to ruin your t-shirt with my bawling when I found out about Temperence. Did you do those things as a manager or as friend?"

She met his challenging stare. "I did as expected."

"So those late, late nights we had. Before my sister ruined whatever was developing, you did it because it was expected of you?" He was glaring at her as if wanting her to remember. She did. When a lull in their conversation about mountains of nothing fell, they would look at each other a second too long, staring at the other's lips. Just right then, Temperance would storm into the room.

"What do you want?" she asked with a loud sigh. "Why are you so obsessed with what I do?"

"You can't guess?" he snarled back. "Come on."

"I don't want to know." Carmen declared defiantly. "I don't need to know to do my job. I don't want you thinking I need to know because our focus should be getting your career back. I can't be your friend if you want me to do that."

"Why not?"

"Because I don't believe in mixing the personal with the professional."

"Fuck me in the ass and call me Sally, Minx. You're fucking engaged to the guy who used to do my PR."

"We only started dating when Seismic broke up." She pointed out. "And what I do outside of my work is none of your fucking business."

She had to walk past him to leave the kitchen. She was halfway to the bedroom when he called for her to stop.

"Alright. No personal stuff. If you believe that's what we must be, we can get what we both want. I just thought . . . Carmen, I really hope we can be friends. Friendships don't ruin partnerships, Minx." He smirked as he put his hands in the pockets of track pants that she recognized was Tanner's. "It's fucking. And we are never going to fuck, are we?"

"Of course not," she muttered.

"Good. I only thought we could be closer. My time at the retreat has given me a new perspective on things. But I would really like for us to be friends, Carmen. I don't just see you as a manager."

"Tomorrow, I'm going to start making calls," Carmen said suddenly, snapping her fingers. Oh, she liked this where she only ran in two settings, Jackal or Beast. If Ramiro was all Feelings and Connection thanks to the retreat, that was his party, and she didn't want an invitation." And we have to get you all glinty and handsome again."

Ramiro frowned. "What the fuck do you mean?"

"Look at you! You're skinny as a rake and that hair - really, Ramiro, if not for your fucking god-like good looks, I would swear you have fleas. We need to make an appointment for haircut and color."

"Hold on." Ramiro said. "Did you just say I look like a god? And what the fuck is wrong with my hair?"

Carmen looked at the ceiling before lowering her head to stare back at him. "We'll need to get in touch with your old trainer to get you all muscly again. You also need to spend a few days in the sun because you're practically as white as a radish. Then we need to round up the guys and tell them Seismic is back. As for your hair, we need it back to its pretty golden blond color. Oh, I don't know. You're forty-two. You can probably pull off the silverfox look."

She turned to go to her bedroom, muttering about making a list. As she typed the code for her tablet, Ramiro startled her by diving onto her bed and making himself comfortable.

"What the fuck are you doing?"

"Doctor Bear said to wake you every two hours."

"I fail to see why you have to be in bed with me."

"Do you have a guest room?"

"I have a lovely couch."

"Which is too small for me. Nah, I'm sleeping here."

"What?"

Ramiro looked hurt and stacked his palms under his head. "You heard me. Be nice, Carmen. I rescued you from drowning and you repay me by forcing me sleep in that midget couch? What must a man do to earn a night in your bed?"

She was horny and missing Tanner. That's why she thought she heard that very suggestive lilt in his voice. She was projecting her sexual frustration on the nearest available target.

"You can't sleep here with me! I'm engaged!"

"I don't see why not. I respect that ring and you. You, on the other hand . . . "his voice trailed off, and he smiled with irritating innocence at her.

Carmen put her tablet away and stalked to the foot of the bed. "Ramiro, really, isn't it bad enough that I got conked on the head? Is it really so much fun to annoy and torture me?"

He laughed. "More than you think, minx." He patted the space next to him. "Come on, we'll talk about my career later. You need rest. We can watch a movie for another two hours before you can sleep."

"Tanner is not going to like this."

Ramiro made a face. "God. That's why I'm never getting married ever. You start asking permission."

"I am not going to ask his permission!"

"Then what? Tell him that Ramiro Brandt is warming your bed tonight?"

God, Ramiro wouldn't be such an excellent lyricist if he didn't know how to twist words in naughty ways. Carmen grumbled, "No. Of course not."

"I'm just here to protect you and to help you as needed, minx."

"Carmen!" She practically screeched. "My name is Carmen, not minx!"

Ramiro grinned again with his ridiculous, stupid dimples and sparkling emerald eyes. "Are you sure? You certainly act like it. Come to bed, Minx. Oh, but shouldn't you get rid of those cute piercings first? We don't want you screaming awake because they got snagged on a thread or something." He patted the pillows and sighed. "If you ask me, the only good reason for waking up screaming is when you someone is fucking--"

"Finish that sentence and not only will I throw you out, Brandt. I'll tell everyone that the reason you sound so good is because you're a fucking ass."

CHAPTER 8

Who the fuck calls this early in the morning? Carmen wondered irritably as she burrowed deeper into the bed in a futile attempt to escape the ringing phone. Bad enough that the ringtone was another Seismic song. She had also put the phone on vibrate mode, rocking loudly on the table's wooden surface for maximum discomfort. She opened one eye, then another whined,

then reached for it. Still lying on the bed, she brought it to her ear.

"This better be good," she growled.

"Hey."

Carmen's eyes widened. "Tanner."

She started to sit up, and that was when she discovered that Ramiro was sound asleep with his nose smooshed to her ear and the manacle grip of his arm around her waist. It was heavy despite skin and bone, and she had to turn and maneuver it before it was off. But the moment she started moving away, Ramiro, still asleep, grunted and flung his arm back and hauled her to his chest. His lips pressed on her nape, and she froze.

"Carmen?" Tanner sounded a little impatient. "Are you there?"

"Who's that?" Ramiro grumbled, pushing his face against the back of her shoulder. Her body temperature leaped up to several degrees as he nuzzled against it. Still sleepy and confused with the call and her body's reactions, she didn't stop Ramiro's hand from sliding under her t-shirt and cupping her breast. He sighed and kissed her shoulder.

"Who the fuck is that?" Tanner demanded.

Recovering her sanity, Carmen covered the phone and hissed at Ramiro, "Get. Your. Hand. Off. Me."

"Your tits are really small." She heard what sounded like wonder despite his voice being scratchy from sleep. She slapped at his hand, and Ramiro yelped, quickly yanking his hand away. She grabbed her pillow, hit him on the head, and then leaped off the bed. Ramiro groaned and turned away from her, curling into a ball.

"I heard someone, Carmen." Tanner was saying when she brought the phone back to her ear.

"Fucking too early to be working, minx," Ramiro complained.

"What the hell is going on there?"

Torn between confusion and annoyance, Carmen, who was blushing, snapped, "It's Ramiro, alright? Ramiro Brandt. He's here and we're - "

"Don't you fucking tell people where I am, minx."

"Shut up."

"Excuse me?" Tanner said, shocked.

"Not you! God, not you! It's - It's Ramiro. He's here. We've been talking." She glared back at the disgruntled blond god blinking up at her.

"You have a meeting with him at six-twenty-two in the morning?"

Carmen frowned at the phone. "Why are you calling so early?"

"God, minx, really? Will you let me sleep?"

She turned back to Ramiro. His face was pressed on the pillow, and his stupid, hobo hair still looked glorious despite being tangled and mussed from sleep. She frowned at the familiar gray t-shirt he was wearing. "Will you shut up? My fiancé is on the line!"

Ramiro snorted. "Ramiro Brandt sends his regards."

"Hold on. Are you telling me that Ramiro Brandt is with you? Where are you?" Tanner asked.

Keeping the phone pressed to her ear, Carmen tripped and staggered to the sliding glass doors that led to the hot tub. A shiver ran up and down her spine before it spread in her entire body as the cold morning mist hit her. She was wearing only a tissue-thin t-shirt and boxers. Wrapping an arm around herself, she spoke to Tanner.

"I'm at home. Ramiro came by early because he's out of rehab and wants his career back," she told Tanner, sitting on a padded lounge chair bathed in soft sunlight. The slight warmth melted off some of the chills from her legs. She rubbed them vigorously for more warmth.

"A bit unorthodox, the idea of a rock star awake at sunrise," Tanner remarked. "I thought you - well - "

Frowning, she asked, "What?"

"Never mind. I called to check on you."

"If you are calling to check on me, you sure took your time. I got only your voice mail last night." Carmen didn't believe in drama, much less throwing a hissy fit. "Why didn't you call or text earlier? I hit my fucking head, Tanner. I was unconscious for a few seconds. I was in the hospital."

"Well, I'm calling now, aren't I? Besides, I had to screen my calls last night, Carmen. Everyone wants everything they could get about Tina. We've released a statement but you know how those sons of bitches are."

But Carmen was not a forgiving woman. Not now, anyway. "You could have sent me a message."

"I told you. I couldn't. After releasing a statement, I had everything go to voice mail. I was exhausted."

"And what is it that you thought was happening earlier when you called?" She pressed, raising an eyebrow.

"Huh? What do you mean?"

"When you said how it's unorthodox for a rock star to be awake. You said you thought something of me. What is it."

Tanner sighed. "Carmen."

Her expression was stony. "Tanner."

"Please don't ruin this, alright? We've only just started talking again."

"I'm not the one with these thoughts. Tell me exactly what you were thinking." As she spoke, she heard the doors parting open. Out sauntered Ramiro, yawning hugely. He raised his t-shirt and scratched his flat stomach, the other arm stretching up.

"Look, I'm sorry, alright? But we haven't really spoken in weeks and I shouldn't have thought you're with another guy."

"I can't believe you! You really think I'd go and fuck someone just because we haven't been okay for a while?"

"Carmen." Tanner sounded tired. "I said I'm sorry."

"It's not enough. I've been in hell thinking of us, wondering why the fuck I'm so hesitant about setting a date and you're thinking the worst of me?" Her lower lip trembled. "You don't trust me."

"That's not true."

"No, you don't."

"I trust you. I swear to god."

"You're an atheist. Don't fuck me, Tanner."

He sighed. "The second I thought it was, it was gone, alright? I know it was wrong. I'm sorry. I don't know how to make that any more clear."

Carmen stared woodenly back at Ramiro, who was still scratching his stomach. Then he started beating his chest and started yodeling.

"What the fuck is that?"

"We'll talk when you get home."

"Carmen - "

She pressed the button to end the call. Ramiro finished beating at his chest and now did what looked like toe touches. The threadbare fabric of the track pants he wore stretched tautly across his firm buttocks, and she rolled her eyes. She stormed back to the bedroom, tossed her phone on the bed, and went to the kitchen.

Trust Tanner to think so low of her because they've been arguing for a while. Carmen's throat was tight as she pulled out food from the cupboard and the fridge without seeing them. It hurt that he had so little faith in her. It probably wouldn't sting so much if this was the first time it happened. Still, he had questioned her commitment and accused her of not taking their relationship seriously for too long already. And now this. Carmen choked back a sob as she got a skillet and fired up the stove. Her breath shook as she swallowed the sobs threatening to rise from her throat.

She was cursing all men when another of their ilk showed up. As infuriating as ever, Ramiro wore an ear-to-ear grin as he drummed his fingers on the counter. He looked well-rested and alert, better despite his tousled hair and beard. He sat down and beamed at her.

"Good morning, minx."

Without another word, she stared at him and put slices of bacon in the skillet. His behavior had been annoying, but that was Ramiro being Ramiro. He would perish if unable to mock or make somebody into a joke. She was used to it. Tanner thinking so awful of her was a knife twisting slowly in her heart.

"So I'm handsy during mornings," Ramiro said, shrugging. "It's a thing. Just ask Robin."

"Ramiro, I really don't have time for your jokes or any of your signature mockery. My head has finally stopped hurting although god only know how much coffee I'll need to survive today because you fucking woke me up every hour last night when it should have been two."

"Two hours felt too long."

"Next time, do as the doctor said."

"That makes sense. They're paid to tell us how to delay death a little longer. And it works."

Carmen snorted and watched the bacon cook. She felt Ramiro approach her before she scented the slight, faded note of soap from his shower last night. With a hand at the small of her back, he put his lips to her ear and said surprisingly gently, "Let me take care of this."

She was still frowning as his fingers pried hers off the spatula, making her shiver and sweat simultaneously at the no-nonsense touch. His eyes looked at her kindly for the first time since last night. Carmen was a sucker for the smallest gestures of such and knew it. Biting her lip, she turned away and busied herself with making coffee.

No word passed between them, except when she asked Ramiro if he wanted to try cinnamon in his coffee. He nodded, then cracked eggs over the pan, where the bacon was sizzling to a beautiful, golden crisp. As coffee streamed down the pot, Carmen poured water and watched with blank eyes. The kitchen was warm and homey with the aroma of bacon, cinnamon, and coffee. They saw through their tasks as if this was another morning of doing them.

She didn't know what Ramiro overheard and was grateful he didn't bring it up. But whatever he picked up on told him she needed comforting right now. At least, that's what she thought when he pressed a hand at the back of her waist as she put plates on the table. His touch was fleeting but warm, and she felt it more profound than her skin. She glanced at him and lowered her eyes when he tucked a tendril of her hair behind her ear. When she looked at him, she saw a little frown forming, and he kissed her on the cheek. Then he was off to finish cooking before her mind registered what had happened.

Ramiro served her first, piling eggs and bacon on her plate before putting the rest on his. He sat down next to her as quickly as if it was something he had always been doing. Carmen picked up a strip of the meat and took a bite. Ramiro watched her chew as he held the coffee poised to his lips.

"How is it?"

She grinned and got another, dipping it in the egg yolk. "You have a bright future as a line cook."

He chuckled and sipped his coffee. "I'll make note of it."

Quieter fell between them. Ramiro watched the flutter in Carmen's lashes as her thoughts returned to the early phone call. He tried to keep his glance casual, but when her cheeks bloomed a lovely pink color, he couldn't look away. Carmen put her cup down, her furrowed eyebrows indicating tension. Realizing she was lost in her thoughts, she snapped out of it and turned to Ramiro. He was swirling his eggs and bacon around the plate with a fork.

"What are your plans today?" Ramiro asked, eating.

"Too many," she answered with a sigh. "Don't you have any?"

Ramiro shrugged. "I've been off the radar for a year. Who do I have to see?"

Realizing what he meant, she said slowly, "Robin doesn't even know you're back."

"I'll tell him tomorrow. Or next week. Once he knows, Father will know. I would rather delay it for as long as I could, minx."

She understood. Scott Brandt was a terrifying man. She had met him once and found him cold and calculating. Robin and Ramiro must have gotten their attitude from their mother.

71

"I also have to start looking for an apartment, check myself in at a hotel while I'm at it."

Carmen loaded egg and bacon on her fork. "What happened to your penthouse and your home?"

"I had the penthouse put on lease so that white elephant would be of some use. At my instructions, Robin sold my place."

"What? So that means - "

Ramiro's smile was rueful as he refilled his coffee. "I'm homeless. I've become the ultimate cliché for a has-been."

"You are not," Carmen declared vehemently. "We'll get you back on top, Ramiro. It will be a steep climb but you have my word you'll be back there, as you should be."

As she spoke, her hand fell on his wrist. Ramiro stared at it, and she flushed, quickly taking it away.

"Seismic is the best rock band, hands down." She stammered, scrambling for something to say. "You guys deserve only the best comeback."

"What have they been up to?"

Lennon and Caitlin were expecting their first child. They had all gone into record producing. Only Euan straddled responsibilities onstage and behind the scenes as he had many musical collaborations. "We've been approached to be coaches for this new reality show about the next big rock band," she told Ramiro as they were washing the dishes. "I'm still thinking about it, but I hear Euan is on."

"Why the hesitation?" Ramiro asked as she passed him the plate to be wiped dry. "I can imagine they're ready to make any deal you want, Carmen."

"I know, and it's exciting. But I don't have the drive to help build a group from the ground up. I'm also enjoying my gig in the magazine and I'll be finishing college in the next semester." At Ramiro's surprised glance, she blushed. "It's no big deal. I've been attending night classes off and on, and it's just community college."

"Yeah. I remember. I just didn't realize how important finishing is for you."

"I know it seems silly," she confessed, feeling her neck warm. "I mean, I'm clearly comfortable with life and I can do whatever I want but it means a lot to have my name on something I worked on myself. And I promised my Dad I'll finish school no matter what."

"Of course. I understand that." He smiled at her fondly. "Well, I'm proud of you."

Carmen flushed and grunted, "And?"

"And I *am* proud of you, minx. You fulfilled your promise to your father against all odds."

They stared at each other. Ramiro's expression was unreadable, and her face reddened by the second. She was the first to look away, hurriedly rinsing her hand and then wiping them dry.

"Ramiro, I have a full day but there are things we have to do." She said briskly as she walked out of the kitchen. Ramiro was following close behind. She turned and almost smacked into him. Blushing again, she cleared her throat. "You are in dire need of a haircut, for one."

Ramiro rolled his eyes and ran a hand through his luscious golden locks. "What? I like my hair like this."

"You look like a homeless person. Which you are, come to think of it."

"I'm a Brandt." He said huffily.

She cocked an eyebrow. "You look like a homeless Brandt."

"That's a first. Don't take that honor away from me." He said, touching his hair again.

"Fine. It's your hair. But we also need to fatten you up, get you to the gym." Carmen stalked to the bedroom, Ramiro once again following her. To her surprise, the bed was fixed, sheets tucked hospital corner tight. Continuing, her tone with a hard, stubborn edge, she said, "And if you're going to stay here, we'll have to find a room for you."

Ramiro made a face but said. "I'm sure I can endure the couch."

"No. I'll have to move some things around in the study but I'm sure I can fit . . . a futon in there." This time, Carmen was red down to her chest, she was sure.

"Minx, please don't put yourself out. I can stay in a hotel - "

"Is that what you'd like?"

Ramiro looked doubtful. "At some point I'll have to be on my own."

"If you're staying here - "

"I told you. Hotels are fine."

"And if you start drinking again? I refuse to have it on my conscience if you revert to that."

"You don't believe in me?" He demanded.

"I never stopped believing in you, Ramiro. But it's a little hard to keep faith when you yourself won't."

He was about to say something, but her words surprised him. When he remained quiet, she continued ticking off plans for today.

"I have meetings until this afternoon and there's this concert I have to go to. But I have two hours free. We can go shopping for the futon then. And, uh, did you pack clothes?"

"The retreat will send me the rest of my stuff."

"We'll see if you you'll survive wearing synthetic fabrics for a day," she told him, grinning. "But until we get you some shirts and pants, I guess we'll be sharing clothes." They were both broad-shouldered, though hers were more impressive. She was six-foot-three, and he an inch shorter. Her t-shirt looked much better on him than on her, and she entertained the image of Ramiro wearing one of her blouses. No doubt he would be way prettier. It wasn't an upsetting thought. His legs would look lovely in her stilettos too . . .

Ramiro smiled back. "Even your underwear?"

"Don't ruin the moment, Ramiro."

AT NOON, CARMEN LEFT HER CAR AT THE VALET SERVICE OF THE HOTEL. The doorman recognized her. Tipped his hat at her. Though she had been there many times, he quickly called a concierge to bring her to the restaurant. The host greeted her and personally brought her to the table where Euan Estrada was waiting.

His hair was a thick, silver-blond, and his eyes a dreamy violet. He was tall and lean and looked and acted every inch like a dreamboat. He rose as Carmen neared the table, his movements more graceful than smooth. His smile was warm as he took Carmen by the hand, and they kissed briefly on the lips. It was an intimate but friendly kiss. Carmen flushed at realizing eyes were watching them, and she fumbled as the host pulled out the chair for her to sit down. Euan followed and regarded her, his gaze curious.

"So he's back," he said without preamble.

Carmen nodded. While Ramiro was in the shower this morning, she made a quick call to Euan, informing him about the return of his best friend. She knew Ramiro wouldn't like what she had done, but she had to know if everyone would be on board with plans for a comeback. A year may have only passed, but it was enough time for fame to fade away and people to forget. The task Ramiro wanted of her was equivalent to launching a new group, except she had people's memories and sentimentality to work with.

Euan and Ramiro were best friends. They made the best collaborators. Though they both wrote songs, Euan was stronger at the lyrics and Ramiro at singing. Euan had been upset that Ramiro quit the band and made Carmen break the news to them. A quiet, introspective man, Carmen saw a rare flare of temper in his eyes upon being told of Ramiro's betrayal.

"I thought you should know first," Carmen told him. "But please don't tell him about this meeting?"

"Of course. You know you can count on me."

A server approached them with menus and a wine list. Euan ordered them, and Carmen just let him do it. She was more concerned with the outcome of this meeting than what she'd be putting in her stomach.

"I know you don't want him to know," he told her when the waiter left. "But I had to tell the rest of the guys." To Carmen's surprise, he was quick to explain. "I thought to spare you. Both of you. Ramiro is like a brother to me. Though he was a self-centered fuck for what he did, I've forgiven him. Lucas, can be persuaded. Lennon would tell whatever Caitlin tells him to do and we both know what that would be. But Russell is another matter."

"Russell," Carmen echoed. "Why?"

"He doesn't want to come back. Ever."

"What?" Carmen exclaimed so loudly that heads turned toward them. He winced as she blushed, and she said more softly, "Explain to me."

"He's tired. He's sick of paparazzi chasing him, sick of the constant violation of his privacy. He's in France and has no plans of returning anytime soon. Not to mention that his family still gives him grief though it's been years since he last saw any of them."

Thrown by this unexpected turn, Carmen found herself grasping at straws. "Maybe if I talk to him - "

Euan shook his head.

"If Ramiro were - "

"Russell absolutely refuses to discuss anything more about the band. He wanted me to make it clear to you."

"What about you and the others?" When Euan remained silent, Carmen's hand flew to her mouth.

"Oh my god." She gasped. "You don't want to revive Seismic anymore."

Euan smiled sadly. "It might be stupid, Carmen, but I'm more satisfied collaborating with other artists and producing music. I didn't have much opportunity for that before. And I can't stomach the idea of Seismic performing with another drummer, no matter how good the guy is. None of us want to. We are Seismic and no one else."

Ramiro was fucked. They both were.

It wouldn't be so upsetting if only it was the best kind of fuck.

CHAPTER 9

Two weeks had passed since Carmen, Tanner, and Ramiro started co-habiting. Finding a futon that would accommodate Ramiro's tall form took them a day and a half. Carmen loathed to have him sleep with her again, but at least Ramiro insisted on taking the couch that night. She wondered whether there was any wisdom at all in her offer that he stay. Conscience and her strict sense of responsibility would trump her doubts. It didn't matter that Ramiro could afford a castle or two in a snap, coming from old money and being rich alone. She wouldn't be at peace leaving him alone, even if he could be prideful and insist he was alright.

Especially given that she had this fucking secret that could either undo him or, best case scenario, encourage him to get back in the game on his own. There was no good way to tell him, but the clock was ticking. The longer she kept it to herself, the worse it would get, and the very thing she was trying to help Ramiro from not doing might happen.

Tanner, as expected, was far from pleased that she had taken in a guest on an indefinite stay. He was once again Ramiro's PR. Despite the buttload of money in it, he did not relish that he lived with work twenty-four-seven. Carmen dreaded when he brought up the subject of their wedding date again. They were talking again, but there was a definite strain as each tiptoed around the other. Except for a perfunctory kiss on her lips when he returned from the trip, they still hadn't touched each other nor talked beyond, "Pass the salt, please."

Ramiro at least had toned down his way-too-playful behavior around her. However, the damned man would still call her minx when they were alone.

On Friday night, he surprised her with the announcement that he was off to have dinner with Robin. Tanner was in an event, and Carmen thought that with just her and Ramiro around, she could finally drop the bombshell about Seismic. She looked at him with relief and uncertainty as he stood before her, looking like his old self again.

His hair was trimmed now but still longish and, having gone through professional treatments, looked more golden and softer. He was clean-shaven though a stubble had begun to grow and outline his elegant, sharp jawline that would be shaved come morning. He was dressed in a dark green button-down shirt, gray slacks, and gleaming Oxfords and was slipping on a matching jacket as he spoke. Carmen's stare lingered on his broad shoulders, a catch in her throat. She looked away as he finished straightening the coat and turned to her.

"That's great," she managed to say and resumed slicing carrots. Then she paused and looked at him. "But . . . where, exactly?"

He smirked. "Why, out in public, of course."

"You don't want anyone knowing you're back and now you want to be seen? Oh," she grunted, realizing that this was his intent. She turned pink as Ramiro spread his palms and gave her a serene, knowing look. "Hey, I can call the paps on you; just say the word."

"Maybe when Robin and I are done with dinner. Of course the servers will be talking." Ramiro said. "Sorry you had the salon people sign NDAs for naught."

"It brought you several days. It's your call, Ramiro. I only do as you ask."

She resumed slicing vegetables, unaware that his gaze was warm on the fall of her hair, a practical bob she never let grow past her ears. Her nape had a surprisingly elegant curve despite her thick, muscular neck. He watched the lightning-quick motions of her hands cutting up vegetables and setting them aside.

"I missed Robin. Hey, you haven't seen him for a long time. I know you're one of the few people my brother actually likes. Why don't you join us?"

"You haven't seen each other in a year. You have a lot to catch up on. I'll just be in the way." Carmen set reached for the bundle of broccoli next. "Next time."

"On the contrary, minx, you are the way in more things you can imagine," he told her. Suddenly, a dark look settled on his handsome face, but it vanished quickly. "I forget. You and Tanner have plans?"

She hoped he stayed out late, actually. Without Ramiro around, Tanner would insist they talk about the wedding. "You can say that. He won't be back for a couple of hours. Don't worry about me. I'll be fine. I have my beef stir-fry and a good book."

"You sure?"

"Positive. Give Robin my love."

Ramiro grinned. "I'll give him your regards, minx."

"Take my car," she offered.

"I was going to call a service so. . thank you?" Then Ramiro went around to kiss her on the cheek. "I'll see you when I get back."

Carmen stared at the front door long after he had gone. She resumed making herself dinner, mixing herbs and spices into the food until she was satisfied with the savory aroma permeating the kitchen. She was going through the wine rack, picking out a bottle, when she heard a car pull up in front. Then the front door was opened, and Tanner was there.

"Hey," he said, nodding at her.

"Hi." Carmen was startled. "You're home early."

"I skipped the party and did some work in the office instead," Tanner replied, shooting her a quick smile. "That smells good. Is there enough for me?"

"Of course there is. Let's eat at the counter?"

"Love it. Just let me change out of this."

Carmen set the table. She kept glancing at the bedroom door as she did, willing herself to relax. She was pouring wine into glasses when Tanner returned to the kitchen. He looked relaxed and younger than his forty-three years in a worn white t-shirt and faded cargo shorts. Carmen smiled at him almost shyly. Encouraged, his black eyes sparkled as he went to her.

They sat down, and Carmen put food onto his plate before hers. As she did, Tanner said, "It's been so long since we sat down for a meal together."

"What do you mean? We have breakfast together." She said, digging into her food.

"Yeah, but something like this. You and me just like this. And not having to rush anywhere. Alone." He added pointedly. She flushed and hid her burning cheeks by sipping wine. "Where's Ramiro, anyway?"

"Out."

"Good."

Then he wrapped an arm around her waist and kissed her.

Carmen sighed against his tongue as they kissed, her hand rising to touch his cheek while he held her. God, it had been so long. She moved so she was closer and could deepen the kiss. How she had missed this. The flavor of his tongue reminded her of spice and impulse. Her fingers thrust through the thick curls of his hair.

Suddenly, Tanner was standing, the chair falling back to the floor with a slam. He grabbed her with him before pressing her against the wall. He grinned at her, and she returned it before she cupped his face again for a kiss. His fingers slipped inside her shorts and dragged the garment down.

The next instant, she was yanked from the wall and pushed against the table. His hand pressed low on her back as he urged her to bend over while the other dragged her shorts down to her legs. She tried turning, wanting to look at him, and tell him to take it slow, but he pushed her back down. Her hands struggled for friction on the smooth surface until she settled for just gripping the edges, her arms flung to the sides as Tanner pushed her down once again, then thrust.

"Wait - "she gasped, her legs closing on instinct as he pushed in. Her head was still reeling from the kiss, and it felt heavy and hot, but the rest of her body hadn't caught up yet. She wasn't that wet. But Tanner spread her legs open from behind and resumed fucking her, his thrusts short and desperate. She grimaced and struggled to push her hand down, fingers arrowing toward her clit. There. The moisture was beginning to gather, easing the piercing discomfort, but she was still trying to turn around.

She hated fucking in this position. She was ugly, she knew that and accepted it, but she wanted to be looked at when fucked. Wanted the man to know he was fucking her and not imagining someone else. Tanner's hand on her back kept her pressed on the table, and it hurt her breasts as the curves and filigrees of her nipple piercings dug and threatened to cut through her skin. She pushed up, and Tanner grunted, his hands sliding to her hips to grip her there as he finished with a rough groan.

Carmen pushed him away as he collapsed on her and yanked her t-shirt down. Tanner sank on one of the chairs and panted, his cock hanging semi-hard between his legs. Carmen wrenched her shorts on, strode to him, and slapped him right in the face.

Tanner nearly fell off the chair. "What the fuck was that for?" He shot back angrily.

But Carmen was more pissed. "What the fuck was that? You know I don't like fucking that way!"

"Oh, I'm sorry for forgetting." Tanner snapped in a tone that conveyed otherwise. He jerked his shorts back up and glared at her. "We haven't fucked in so long I forgot."

"Sometimes you're shit at lying, Tanner."

Carmen refused to step aside when he shot to his feet, so his shoulder collided with her chest. She glared after him as he stalked.

"Don't you walk away from me. Don't you fucking walk away from me!"

"Really, Carmen?" Tanner turned around mockingly. "I figured since you do it so much it's time I know how fun it is for you."

"What's wrong with you? Why won't you talk to me?"

"Talk to you! How when you're always running away!"

She flushed, unable to deny it. Seeing that he'd made a dent, Tanner smirked.

"You brought this upon yourself."

Blue eyes flashed. "Son of a bitch."

"I don't know if it's escaped your notice, my dear sweet fiancée," Tanner spat. "But if you notice, we're nowhere near setting a wedding date. Just when I thought we could finally fix this shit we've been wading in for months, you went right ahead and took on that Ramiro Brandt had him fucking living here in our house without even talking to me first!"

Carmen responded with the first thing that came to mind. "This is my house."

"Yes! This is *your* fucking house! I sleep in *your* fucking bed. I fuck you on *your* sheets, on *your* couch, in *your* kitchen. The only place for me is your cunt."

Carmen, disgusted at the turn of their discussion, turned to leave. Tanner roared.

"Fucking walk away from me this time and we're over."

She whirled around. First, she paled, then her face warmed as a look of utter shock settled there. It transformed into outrage, one she could barely control, given her thick lower lip trembled.

And then a sea of calm began to rise inside her. It was still and quiet, freezing the cracks in her heart yet strengthening a resolve she didn't know she had until that moment. Suddenly everything was so clear. She no longer willed herself to blindness.

"Haven't we been for a long time?" She whispered.

"You did this."

"No." Her voice was calm. "You did."

Tanner shook his head. "All I want is to love you and marry you, Carmen. Make you mine at last."

"I've always been yours, Tanner, and I don't doubt you want to marry me. But love me?" She made a tutting sound, walking around him like a predator eyeing her prey. "You don't."

He looked at her. "Really. The man who wants to marry you doesn't love you."

"How can you think I don't know?"

"What are you talking about?" He snapped.

"All my life people didn't think much of me. I will always be that ugly, waste of space. No matter how much I have. So I made myself into the person people would respect. If not that, then feared." Carmen put one foot in front of the other as she went to him. "I own this town, Tanner. What do you think that means?"

He stared back at her wordlessly, swallowing. His black eyes betrayed nothing but his entire body was tight with tension.

Carmen sighed, looked around, and found her phone on the counter. She scrolled until reaching the Gallery folder and opened it. She stared at the photos there, images forever seared and carved in her mind despite the time passed.

"I work hard. I got here knowing that it was due to my hard work and people who have helped me. The general manager of Bloom Hotel was my boss when I used to wait tables in high school." She said casually. "He wrote my recommendation for college, basically gave me all these lessons on how to get to the top. You can say he was like a father to me. So he thought it prudent for me to know the sort of man I was going to marry."

Without warning, she tossed her phone to Tanner, who caught it. Her eyes rested on him, her face looking serene, as he watched the slide show of photos of him entering and exiting a room with different women.

She bit her lip as ice settled and began seeping into her heart's raw wounds.

"I couldn't believe it. I should have confronted you but I was afraid that either you'd lie and I'd believe it or you would admit to it and I lose you. I loved you and needed you, and I wanted so much to be with you. I have eyes and ears everywhere, Tanner, whether I like it or not. And those eyes and ears are loyal to me. I forgave the first indiscretions because I loved you and . . . you asked me to marry you. I thought . . . But then I got that . . . I wanted so much to be proven wrong but I couldn't be. Now I know why I can't marry you, Tanner." She let out a long, resigned sound. "It's my fault. I should have confronted you. Less afraid of losing you but I loved you. I can't have total trust you. I don't think I do. And now I can't stomach having you in my life."

Tanner flung her phone to the table with a force that had it smashing into pieces. But Carmen didn't flinch.

"Like you weren't going around spreading your legs for another."

Confused, she stared back at him. His grin was evil.

"I know for a fact that you slept with Ramiro Brandt."

"Never," she growled.

"No? Then why did my pillow smell like him when I got back?" At her shock, he chuckled. "Try lying your way out of this one. I could smell him everywhere in that bed."

This time Carmen lost it. "Because I fucking had a concussion and had to be woken up every two hours! He stayed with me to do that. Don't liken me to you, you fucking bastard. I was willing to stay in this relationship, I wanted to marry you but I was this stupid fuck thinking stupidly that you'd tell me about those women. I was so fucking stupid to worry about losing you when you're not worth keeping at all."

"That's rich coming from you. You just strung me along. Do you have any idea what I had to do to be with you?"

"I didn't force you to sell your place. You wanted to live here."

Tanner slapped his palm on the table with satisfaction. "And there you go. I was always the one wanting to be with you."

Carmen crossed her arms. "That what you were thinking when you fucked Tina Hanson's personal assistant?"

But Tanner wasn't listening. "It was always me wanting to move forward with you. Me. You wouldn't sleep over at my place so I had to show how much I wanted to be with you. When I asked you to marry me and you still wouldn't do that, I practically had to beg to live with you."

"Are you trying to justify why you were fucking other women? That this was all my fault? Did I hold a gun to your cock and told you to fuck elsewhere?"

Tanner threw her a look of dark disdain and stormed out of the kitchen. Carmen heard him ripping into the closet. Then he was out an overnight case in hand. He cast another look of utter hate at Carmen, who only stared back calmly.

"Make sure that's all your things," she said. "I'm changing locks and fuck you if you think I'll ever let you back in here."

CHAPTER 10

The waitress was a slim, curvy brunette whose smile never faltered the entire night. It had a hopeful lilt, matched with eyes that simmered with lust. In return, Ramiro sent her a dry expression while Robin struggled to mock his big brother.

"Can I interest you with dessert?" She spoke to both but at the last word, stared at Ramiro.

"Just bring us coffee," Robin answered when Ramiro looked away from her, hiding his annoyance. The girl huffed for the first time in the night, realizing that the handsome Brandt brother was not into her. She muttered something about getting their order and walking away.

"So she does walk normally," Ramiro retorted, turning back and grunting under his breath. "I thought those hips were going to pop off with the way she was swaying."

"Be nice," Robin told him. "She can't help putting the moves on you. You are, after all, annoyingly handsome."

Ramiro snorted and brought a glass of water to his lips. "Not my type."

Robin rolled his eyes. "Since we've sat down, a redhead model whom I heard isn't particularly choosy with who she fucks made eyes with you until she left with someone else. A blond who had the guts to send you a drink inviting you to join her at the bar, and probably the most beautiful woman of the night, with a downright sexy accent came right up to us, at this table." He tapped it with his chubby finger for emphasis, "and said she would do me if you'd do her. And now that waitress looks like she will be amenable to *anything* in bed. What do you want?"

"I don't believe my manager would approve of me starting an affair with anyone when she's working day and night trying to get me back on top," Ramiro drawled. He continued to stare at Robin, who ignored him and smiled at the frowning brunette. She served them their coffee, parroted the standard, "Enjoy your coffee," put on a fake, painful smile then left. Ramiro let out an impatient sigh while Robin chuckled.

"Oh, I never thought I'd see the day when Carmen Schwartz quite literally holds you by the cock, brother," he said. "I wonder what our dead sister would say about that."

Ramiro shot him a warning glance before putting cream in his coffee. "You sure know how to ruin the night."

"I thought you've dragged that woman by the roots," Robin said, ignoring his temper. "She's not worth another thought, you know that."

"She's our sister."

"More yours than mine."

Ramiro sighed. "I'm here tonight to see you and show you I'm alive. Not to talk about her."

"Fine. Fine. If not Temperence, then let's go back to Carmen. Since when did your manager had a say on where you put your cock?"

Robin's favorite jokes involved sex, and there was no better audience than his brother. Ramiro could dish it back, but tonight, though it wasn't Robin's intent, he couldn't. Not when he imagined Carmen panting in his ear, her big hands eagerly guiding his cock to her cunt. His cock twitched, picturing her hard thighs pinning him down, totally enslaving him with her beautiful eyes and star nipple piercings. He couldn't get over the image of her nipples looking pink and swollen, gleaming with the piercings from the water.

His fascination with Carmen had been going on for as long as he could remember. She was ugly and often wore a surly expression, making her astonishingly beautiful eyes look wrong on her face. She could be the most unpleasant company since she was always herding the band like cattle and imposing limits on their fun. They all rebelled at her putting them on schedule - up at dawn for a workout, a strict diet that only allowed one meal for indulgence, practices, and rehearsals. She was a hard-ass but delivered results.

And when she wasn't being a manager, she was a good, trusted friend, if not an ally. Ramiro would never forget the added security she placed around Russell when his family would try to sneak into their concerts and hurl abuse at him. Aware of her influence as the manager of the biggest rock band ever, she had gone on record to denounce the spread of hate, intolerance, and bigotry. The Alliance for Values and Morals then went on the attack, filing a motion for songs by Seismic and other similar groups and artists to be banned for encouraging depravity among the young. Ramiro was called to testify, but his inherent need to mock got him thrown out. Carmen's testimony not only painted the Alliance as idiots but also put Seismic records and other songs back on the market.

He had to go away for a year and lose her to another man to realize he loved her. Not in love. But love her. Truly, madly, deeply.

When she told him the year before that she was engaged, Ramiro was devastated. His sister was gone, his guilt over her death gnawing at him non-stop. Now the one pillar of light in his life was gone, lost to a man worthy of her. Ramiro couldn't like Tanner because he thought

PR guys were shallow. Still, following her announcement, he realized he would have to accept the other man in her life or lose her completely. Tried. He tried but couldn't.

When he realized that nothing was holding nor keeping him anymore, no band, no Carmen, no nothing, he set out to heal himself. He went to the retreat to recover from his addictions and deal with Temperence's ghosts, but most of all forgot Carmen.

Again, he tried.

Really tried.

Now he was living with her, and she shared her bed with that other man. Haunted by the idea that Tanner would fuck his lady love senseless, Ramiro thought about taking sleeping pills. Just thought. His solution was some heavy-duty earphones for when they would fuck. He dreaded sleeping at night, snapping awake whenever he heard a groan or a squeak from the mattress next door. He heard nothing. Still, he wasn't in the house all the time. Who's to say they didn't sneak back in and fucked on the couch?

But Ramiro realized he would probably survive hearing Carmen moaning and screaming when Tanner fucked her. Being married to him - that he couldn't.

Ramiro knew that wealth and good looks wouldn't move Carmen. He liked to think that he may have been in love with him if not for Temperence's presence when he slayed songs with his golden voice, and people worshipped him. That was the best of him, and that's what she was going to get. He did miss singing and performing. He missed Seismic but nothing compared to the hole in his heart at the thought of losing Carmen for good. That would not be warm-hearted. He knew he wasn't going to survive that.

"Since I promised her not to get home very late," Ramiro answered smoothly, checking on his watch. "I have to go."

"Go? Ramiro, it's ten-thirty. Did Carmen impose a curfew on you?" Robin demanded in disbelief. "Bloody hell, that woman is a fucking control freak. Don't tell me she's got her own bowel movements scheduled too? And yours?"

"Wouldn't put it past her." Ramiro answered with a smile, imagining himself and Carmen in the shower. "Come on, I'll take care of this."

He doled out bills from his wallet, and they stood up. All eyes were on them when they were first led to the table. Ramiro rolled his eyes, annoyed. Robin walked ahead, chin up and his expression smug. Ramiro shuffled after him.

"Father would be summoning you next," Robin said as they stood in front of the restaurant waiting for valet.

"You really can't not tell him?" Ramiro asked with a wince.

Robin was sympathetic but shrugged. "Who's to say no one there took a snap of you? And those sharks." He nodded at the paparazzi beginning to approach them.

"Hell, "Ramiro muttered, ushering Robin back inside the restaurant. "I told her to wait until we're done."

"Carmen's only doing what you told her," Robin pointed out.

"That she does. Doesn't mean I have to like it." Ramiro turned away from the glare of the flashbulbs.

The valet arrived with the car. Ramiro and Robin ran for it, ignoring the shouts and calls from the paparazzi to give them a nice photo. Someone shouted, "Imp!"

As Ramiro gunned the engine, Robin stuck his head out the window and yelled, "My cock is still bigger than yours!"

They laughed as Ramiro drove away from the restaurant, quickly shifting gears. "I missed you, baby brother," he said, glancing at Robin with a warm smile before turning back to the road.

"Missed you too." Robin said. "Ah, the brothers, back in action."

"I can't wait to be in a recording studio again," Ramiro admitted. "I've written a lot in the retreat. Until now, too. There's got to be a hit or two in the pile."

"I can't wait to see you back onstage," Robin agreed. "You've always looked good up there. Fuck, it's where you belong."

Ramiro was quiet. "Hopefully that's not only where I belong."

"I'd be happy to find that one cunt that would make my cock sing," Robin said.

Ramiro chuckled. "Thanks a lot for the visual."

"I'm serious!" Robin exclaimed. "I think I've reached my pussy saturation point. I'm not saying no to fucking ever but I'd like to come home to someone. Fuck only that someone. Really, it's so tiring going home with a different woman every night."

"I'm not a woman."

"No, you definitely are not. But you're prettier than Carmen." Grinning mischievously, Robin asked, "So, I know she's engaged to that guy. But have you seen her naked."

She has the sweetest-looking nipples and a full bush. Her cunt is butter-pink. I'd be happy to live the rest of my days on my knees for her." Of course not."

"Why not? With legs like that, she's got to be keeping another treat or two under her pants. God should rue the day pants were invented. Tell Carmen the next time I see her she'd better be in a skirt." Robin smirked. "A mini-skirt."

"Tell her yourself. That would be interesting." Ramiro's smile was genuine. "She's always thought of you as a dirty little lecher."

"I *fucking love* it. Ah, hell, if Tanner Morrison hadn't snapped her up I would. Carmen Schwartz has keeper written all over her."

Ramiro cast him a side-eye. "I don't follow."

"She's certainly dedicated. Just look at you. She's self-made and I believe Father won't scare her off. The way I see it," Robin finished with a shrug, "she's good stock."

"' Good stock,' by the fuck," Ramiro howled. "Did you just hear yourself?"

"There's the fact that if we fuck, we'll populate the planet with our ugly, giant babies."

"Hey." Ramiro frowned at him. "Watch it. That's my - *friend* you're talking about."

"Never thought of fucking her?"

"Come on."

"What? Now that our sister's gone, think of your cock."

"Robin."

"You remember Jaylon?"

"Your leather-faced butler who has to be put in his place?" Jaylon was probably the rudest, most foul-mouthed person Ramiro had ever met. But Robin vowed the man knew how to run and manage a house.

Robin clapped his hands. "I'll be sure to pass that along. Anyway, now that you're back, I'd like to repay the man's good service by, uh, arranging a meeting with your manager and my butler."

"He's a butler. And Carmen's - "Ramiro glared at Robin. "She's engaged, you idiot."

"I'm sure like any other girl she's dreaming of a last free fuck before welcoming matrimony."

"No. If that's your intention, no."

"What if I were to present to her - "

"Robin."

"I'm sure - "

"Don't," Ramiro warned,*" even think about it."*

Robin turned to his brother, about to make a witty comeback. Then he saw the twitch under his cheek, a tell-tale sign of a mounting temper, and the stiff set of his jaw. Robin waited until Ramiro negotiated a problematic turn to his place, then spoke up.

"Ramiro. Do you *like* her?"

"*What?* Fuck, no!"

"Really."

"You're ridiculous."

"No, you are."

"I have no compunction against dropping you off in the middle of nowhere."

"I have my cell phone and my Brandt looks."

Damn.

"So, do you volunteer as Carmen's last free fuck?" Robin prompted.

Ramiro hit the brakes.

CHAPTER 11

R obin wisely shut up for the rest of the drive. Ramiro was grateful. There was no question to how he felt about Carmen, but he didn't want anyone picking up on it first, especially his brother. The relentless teasing was not his main issue. It was that it was knowledge Carmen must know first. He remembered too well what happened the last time someone else realized it.

He dropped off his little brother. As Robin unbuckled his seatbelt, he said, "I apologize for being insensitive."

"There's no need to apologize but next time, just shut up," Ramiro said. Robin nodded. He should have known better than crossing a fellow Brandt. No, Brandt made idle threats. Ramiro had actually stopped the car and ordered Robin out. Robin had laughed before he realized he was serious.

Ramiro left Robin standing at the door of his townhouse. He had a thirty-minute drive ahead of him.

He was eager for home, even if it was with Tanner and Carmen. Propriety and sense told him to make arrangements to move out soon before he overstayed his welcome, but Ramiro was ready to fight. For as long as they were unmarried, he had a chance. He only needed a window. He would have created such a window if he was his old self. Something told him to have faith.

Carmen lived in the suburbs. She hated living in the city and was willing to leave earlier for work. Ramiro, until last year, couldn't imagine living elsewhere. The home was Crowne Estate until college. He returned only once. The quiet life of a town made him uneasy, but after two weeks in the suburbs now, he saw her rationale behind it. It wasn't as soft as he thought, but it helped to distance himself from the city, even by just a few miles. Carmen also lived in a private community, restricting the paparazzi from camping.

Ramiro was cruising on a street where he would have to make the last turn to Carmen's house. Who would he see other than herself? There was no mistaking her for anyone else - he would recognize the tight, athletic shape of her butt anywhere and those legs. Robin might curse for inventing pants but not Ramiro. Not leggings, anyway. Hell, her legs were insanely long. It was dark, and her leggings were black, but he made out every bulge and ripple of muscle in her thighs, her calves.

She was jogging ahead of him, lost in the motion of her legs and feet thudding on the ground. The night was fantastic, but she wore only a faded orange t-shirt, now marked with splotches of sweat on her back. He gently tapped the horn, and she whirled around, her blue eyes wide, then squinting. He quickly lowered the lights as she shielded herself from the glare. Recognition dawned on her face, and she approached him.

Bloody hell. Her hips didn't oscillate in that seductive way women seemed to know, but her strides ate up the ground, and he couldn't look away. He lowered the passenger door's window as she bent at the waist.

"You're home," she said. Her face was red and gleamed with sweat. She looked uglier, and he didn't think that was possible, yet his chest was tight. Her eyes were blue and seemed extra shiny in the night.

The neckline of her t-shirt was high, so that was disappointing. But he smelled her sweat and, dare he say it, moonlight on her skin. It was cool and fresh, touched by her personal musk that had him taking a deep breath to absorb it in his system.

"You're out," he told her. "Can I give you a lift?"

She smirked and opened the door.

"I didn't know you run at night," Ramiro said as he resumed driving. With the window shut, her scent clouded the car. God, she smelled like moonlight and woman. Warm, vital, red-faced woman. He was grateful that his pants were dark, and so was the car, else Carmen would think him a pervert.

"I was feeling restless," was her answer.

He forced a grin. "Tanner isn't distracting enough?"

"He had to leave."

"Oh."

So it was just the two of them tonight.

Ramiro pulled up in her driveway. He followed her out of the car, admiring how the t-shirt, though definitely not her color, fit her. Her waist was not curvy, but she had more muscles than he thought possible. He watched her easily reach the top of the doorway and feel for the key. Under the sleeves of her t-shirt were dark, round patches of sweat.

He saw everything that women hid from men. He knew women sweated but not like Carmen, not like this. Damn, but she was still sweating.

His cock was beginning to hurt really bad.

"How's Robin?" Carmen asked as she unlocked the door and went in. Ramiro followed her, forcing himself to stop leering at her legs.

"Infuriating as ever, but he's blood, so I have no choice but to love him," Ramiro replied as he crashed on the couch. He kicked off his shoes with a sigh, then put his feet up on the coffee table.

Carmen took a bottle of water from the kitchen and drank. He had to look away from the motions of her throat swallowing. When she finished, he turned back to see her returning the drink to the fridge.

"Social media has picked up on your presence," she told him, leaving the kitchen so she could sit on the ottoman across from him. She toed off her running shoes and socks, then put her feet up on the table, her legs resting beside his. God, were those freckles? He thought.

"You really did call the paps on me?"

"It's my job. I'll show you from my tablet but later."

"Where's your phone?"

She blushed, and that intrigued him. "It fell, and it's broken. I'll replace it tomorrow."

"Show me tomorrow. Actually, show me never." Ramiro said, leaning heavily against the couch. "I'd rather read about myself when I've done something worthwhile, not because I've made the first step in bringing the return of the grunge look."

Carmen's laugh was a cross between horsey and a snort. Her eyes looked very blue and bright as they regarded him. "I take back what I thought about your stupid hair. It works."

He grinned. "Told you."

"And you will do something worthwhile, Ramiro. I promise." Then her cheeks warmed again.

Suddenly, she shot to her feet, picking up her shoes and sneakers. Surprised by her sudden reaction, he asked, "What's wrong?"

For the first time since knowing her, a look of uncertainty crossed her features. The amusement in her eyes was replaced with something akin to despair. Ramiro straightened up, tensing.

"I don't know if this is the time to say it," Carmen began, revealing a tremor in her voice. She looked at her bare toes as she spoke. "There is never a good time to say it."

Ramiro couldn't imagine what she had to say that made her look at him like that, almost with fear. Like she had disappointed him. Carmen ran her hand down her stomach when he was looking at her.

"Fuck me hard, minx. Are you pregnant?" He growled, jerking to his feet.

"What? No!" Carmen glared at him. "What the hell?"

"You did this." He mimicked her.

"That's because I didn't have dinner."

"You didn't have dinner and you're off running? What if you fainted? What if you fainted and someone kidnapped you? What kind of *idiot* goes running in the dark starving?" Ramiro ranted, his green eyes staring at her with disbelief.

"Okay, will you sit down?" Carmen asked calmly. She looked somewhat annoyed at the combination of his anger and concern." Because this isn't easy for me."

"Aren't you feeling faint? Why don't you sit down?"

"It's going to take more than a missed meal to put me on my ass, Brandt. Sit. Down."

He glared at her challengingly, and she stared right back. Then he sat back down. Carmen put her sneakers down and sat on the coffee table. She looked worried. As if she was about to relay some horrible news.

"Ramiro, I want you to know that what happens next is entirely up to you. I believe in you. You are so talented," she said

passionately, her eyes seeming to plead with him to believe her. "I hope . . . I hope you don't stop because you are one of the greatest artists of this generation. And I swear to you to bring you back to the top where you belong. That's' where you should be. On top. You're the best and you deserve better. Much better." Suddenly, she burst into tears.

Her face crumpled, rendering her ugly than ever. She couldn't stop getting uglier. Confused but worried for her, he put his hands on her knees and stroked her hard thighs up and down.

"Hey. What's going on exactly, minx?" She let out a loud, broken sob, and he took her chin between thumb and forefinger. Her breath was unsteady puffs from her red nose. He stared at her searchingly, looking into her teary sapphire eyes, her big mouth curved down as she struggled to make more sobs. His other hand climbed to her cheek.

"Stop that. Tell me."

"Don't be angry with me."

"I could never, Minx."

A fresh bout of tears fell down her cheeks.

"Stop calling me that."

Despite his concern, he smiled. "But it suits you."

"Fuck you, Ramiro."

He laughed and wiped her tears away with his knuckles. "How can you think I'll hate you when you're always calling me names and I never once complained about it?"

She sniffed. "This is different."

"Nothing you can do will make me hate you, Carmen." He pushed back the sweaty tendrils of her hair from her forehead as he spoke. "How dare you doubt me." But his voice was gentle, even smiling.

Carmen hung her head. "Oh god."

If he couldn't convince her with words, there was another way.

Ramiro once again took her by the chin so she would look at him. He looked into her eyes at the devastation on her ugly face.

Then he kissed her.

Her lips were soft, but he knew that because of their whole, plump curve. It took everything Ramiro had to keep the kiss quick, too quick, cruelly sharp, lest she thought - well, what would she think? He stopped himself from licking her just in time, pushing himself away from her with painful reluctance. He sat back, his heart a furious thump in his chest as he struggled from licking his own lips to have a taste of her that remained there.

She stared back at him, cow-eyed. He schooled his expression into an unreadable mask.

"See?" He said blandly. "I clearly don't hate you."

"Not yet."

"Why don't you let me prove you wrong."

"Ramiro, we're friends, right?"

He nodded. "Always." His hand fell on her knee, his eyes on her face. "You'll never lose me, minx."

"I would like to believe that."

"Let me prove it to you."

The saddest blue eyes in the world stared back at him.

"Ramiro, there's no Seismic anymore."

Once again, Carmen punched and pushed at the pillow.

Hours had passed since she killed Ramiro's dreams. Hours, but every time she closed her eyes, she saw the flicker of hope vanishing from his eyes. It was awful, just awful. Carmen cursed Euan, Russell, Lennon, and Lucas for putting her in this position. Then she thought about kicking herself because she could have forced them to break the news to Ramiro themselves. They were friends longer. It was their obligation.

She should learn to take on fewer things. Especially those that smashed the spirit.

God, I hate myself.

Carmen gave up on sleep at three in the morning and left bed. It was futile to search the bathroom for sleeping pills because she flushed her prescription down the toilet when Ramiro moved in. The wine was also kept at a minimum but getting drunk was never an option. Milk! She remembered. Warm milk. Maybe with a dash of cinnamon too. That ought to work.

She tried to be quiet, tinkering in the kitchen. She rinsed the saucepan and then put it on the stove. The milk in the fridge was less than half whole, just about to fill a mug. She poured it into the pan, found the cinnamon, and added it.

She was about to bring the mug to her room when a rough groan came from Ramiro's room. She froze. He was struggling to sleep too. So she turned on her heel and tapped softly on his door. A startled, husky voice answered her. "Carmen?"

"Can I come in?"

Much sheet rustling followed. Just when she thought he must have been talking in his sleep, he called for her to come in.

Ramiro had witched the bedside lamp on and rubbed his eyes from the glare. As he removed his hands and looked up at her from the futon, Carmen realized just how much of her he could see for the first time. The lighting may be limited, but there was no disguising the thinness of her t-shirt, that she was wearing only panties though they were the big, full-style grannies favored. Despite clearly sleepy, alertness reached Ramiro's eyes when he stared at her nipples.

"Uh, I have milk." She said, setting it down on the table. "It's yours if you want it."

He sighed and sat up. Carmen looked away from his bare chest and golden hairs scattered on it. The blanket puddled at his trim waist.

"Can't sleep either?"

She looked at her feet, then at him. "I'm so sorry."

"God, fuck, Carmen," Ramiro said impatiently. "I told you none of it is your fault."

She nodded and turned to go.

"You woke me up and now you're just leaving?"

"I have milk." She said, not knowing what else to say.

Ramiro's eyes burned at the sight of her tits before drawling, "Well, if you're offering, bring it over here."

Carmen took the mug and went to him. Ramiro watched her put it on the bedside table, but his hand caught her by the wrist when she turned to go.

"Where are you going?"

"Ramiro, I'm not . . . I'm not really dressed." She was blushing heavily.

He rolled his eyes and released her hand so he could get the milk. "I've already seen you naked, minx. There's no point of hiding yourself from me. Don't leave." He suddenly begged, taking a sip of the milk. Then another. "Fuck, that's good. Sit down, Carmen. No. Not at the foot of the bed. Next to me."

Seeing her dubious stare, he held up his hands.

"I promise I will not take advantage. No matter how tempting you look."

"Tempting." She had to laugh. "Right."

So she sat down. To her surprise, Ramiro put the blanket around her, handing her the mug. "What are you doing?" She demanded

.

"It's cold." He nodded pointedly at her nipples. He grinned. "You want me to warm them up for you?"

"Ramiro." She warned him, hating how taut her body became at his offer.

"Just kidding. Try some of that milk. It's good. What's in it?" He lay back down, turning to look up at her.

"Cinnamon," she added. "I like the smell."

"Finish it," he urged her.

"I should go back - "

"Stay." At her stunned look, he repeated it: "Stay, Carmen. I need my friend."

She knew he didn't desire her, but it just felt wrong in light of what had just happened with Tanner. Yet her body refused to budge an inch away from Ramiro. Instead, it lay down on the futon. It was a tight fit, but after some shifting and turning, their tall, broad forms fit snugly. Carmen put the mug on the nightstand and turned off the light.

"Just for tonight," she told him, her eyes looking at him though she couldn't see him in the dark. But she felt the warmth of his body, the rough hairs of his legs as they tickled her bare ones. She turned on her side, her back against his chest.

Ramiro's voice sounded hollow. "Only tonight."

He put his arm around her waist. Carmen closed her eyes as he kissed her on the forehead.

Moved by his gesture, she whispered, "I believe in you, Ramiro. Always."

Then she dreamed of mighty roars that reached right into her heart.

Her words began stitching pieces of himself that had torn and ragged. He kissed her again, on the shoulder this time, and was finally given the release of sleep.

His dreams were blue, oceans of immeasurable depths and mountains upon mountains of sapphires.

CHAPTER 12

S he knew before coming fully awake that Ramiro's head rested on her chest, his arm and leg clutching her as if she were a lifeline. Her eyes opened, staring sleepily at the pale beams of light streaming through the gap where the drapes had not been pulled wholly closed. Then she looked at the golden head resting between her breasts.

She saw a thick and golden still, now sprinkled with silver in some, tentatively touching them with her fingertips. They felt like silk threads, something to be envied, she thought, her touch acquiring some sureness.

Ramiro let out a breath, and she stilled. He surprised her by murmuring, "Don't stop."

She didn't know if he was awake or dreaming, but she did as she asked.

As she stroked his hair, her mind reeled back to what had been written about Ramiro and what she knew first-hand. He was a tough nut to crack, check. Interviews and profiles that claimed to be in-depth could only get to the heart of Ramiro Brandt. His lyrics showed a man of intelligence but cynical towards the establishment in many things. Interviewing Ramiro was almost disappointing because the things he sang about were precisely what he was. Though he never went on record to explicitly say which songs were directly inspired by personal events, it was well-known that he did get a lot from his life.

In private, Ramiro was more interesting and compelling. He relaxed, and he looked years younger. His in-born snark drove them up the wall, but you could never accuse him of being deceiving. He said exactly what he thought, whether it pleased you or not. But way past that veneer of smug impenetrability was a vulnerable man paralyzed at times by genuine fear.

He constantly worried about disappointing people. Carmen remembered how he couldn't relax during those crucial minutes before a show because Temperance would complain that he was addicted to applause and glory. He never had time for her anymore. Carmen saw that Temperance was disturbingly possessive of Ramiro to the extent that if she had her way, she would manage his career so they were never apart. Robin said they had always been close and bonded even more at the death of their mother. She was sorry for all the time she saw Ramiro conflicted when Temperance pressured him to cut back on performances. Also, the band pressed him to concentrate on them.

Now Temperance was gone.

It was terrible to be glad that someone was dead, no matter how vile she was. Ramiro cared for his sister, protected her, loved her, and took her dead hard. Though he had long dreamed of being free of her, it never crossed his mind that her violent death would pave the way. And if they were that close, Carmen could understand why he did the things he did. She wasn't herself when her father died, as well. At eighteen years old, she lost the one she loved the most.

Ramiro seemed to have forgiven her for abandoning him at his lowest moment. Carmen hoped so, else why did he write to her? Why was he here? And now, trusting her to give him comfort no matter how small. Ramiro tends to ask for so little of himself.

For the first time since telling him the news about Seismic, she realized just how alone he was.

His father, the feared businessman Scott, disowned him for being in a band instead of finishing school. Only when Ramiro proved he could attain success on his own did father and son begin to see each other. Still, he told Carmen he couldn't really forgive his father. Robin at least understood and supported his brother. Still, he wasn't there during the first days of Seismic, those moments when surrendering was the easiest and the best option. Ramiro found himself in music, and it shaped who he was. Now that the band he lived for was gone, Carmen worried he might lose his way again.

Or worse.

She embraced him. To herself, she vowed to never abandon him again.

Ramiro, still half-asleep, sighed and burrowed deeper. He nuzzled her breasts, drawing a soft moan from her. She stiffened, embarrassed by her response. She squeezed her eyes shut, wanting to disappear as she felt Ramiro move, his actions surer and firmer until she felt him leaning up and looking at her.

"Will you let me?"

Startled, her eyes flew open.

He was looking at her with a grave expression as if about to reveal something life-shattering to her. Up close, she saw the lines around his eyes that weren't there a year before. The graceful, natural arch of his eyebrows was more silver. Before she knew what was happening, her hand climbed to his cheek to see the rasp of the stubble. She bit her lip, and she saw his tongue licking his lips. He had gone still as she touched his face.

"You were not this old last year," she said, making a face at how stupid the words sounded.

He smirked as her thumb skated on the groove next to his lips. "I *am* older."

"You have silver. Here," she touched his beard, his eyebrow. "Here."
Then her fingers slid through his hair. "Here. At the top. And only
seen when I'm like this."

He turned his head as her hand lowered to touch the other side of his
face. His breath was warm and shaky. "When you're in my arms?"

She traced his eyebrow. "You're in my arms, Ramiro."

His smile was brighter than the sun entering the room.

"I'm so sorry about last night."

"Damn it, minx. Stop apologizing." Ramiro kissed her fingers and
moved. Carmen moved too, shifting and spreading her legs until he
settled between them. He grinned at the pink spots spreading across
her cheeks as his hardened cock nudged at her. "You didn't end Seismic. You fought to put us back together."

She dropped her hand and looked away. "I failed."

"No."

She turned back to protest. Yes, she did, but Ramiro's lips on hers
stopped her. Shock froze her though his lips were warm, very warm,
and soft, the softest she had kissed. His lips rested on hers for a few
seconds before his head turned. He teased the suddenly-sensitive
corners of her lips, then a tongue joined the game he was drawing her
into, a game in which she had no knowledge of rules and only him.
Yet her hands returned to him, light on his bare shoulders where the
skin was warm and muscles strained and pushed under her palms.

Blood roared in her ears as Ramiro deepened the kiss, a slow, sure
devouring of her mouth, her tongue. He was hard and thrusting
between her legs. Despite the fabric between their bodies, she hissed
at the undeniable bulge pressing and nudging at her pussy. A rough
tingle began between the lower regions of their bodies, and Ramiro
must have felt it, too, because his hips started rocking against hers.
Her legs climbed to his side before her ankles crossed at the middle of
his back.

"Ramiro." She closed her eyes, pulling her mouth away from his kisses. Less than twenty-four hours ago, she was engaged. Shorter than that, Tanner broke her heart. Way faster, she turned around to break Ramiro's. The guilt nagged at her, but his lips brushing random freckles on her cheek, down her neck, pushed this dimness back and back. She was terrified. Not of Ramiro. But because nothing was stopping this now.

No Temperance.

No Tanner.

No guilt.

Her hands grabbed his boxers as Ramiro lowered his head and started mouthing and licking her tits through her t-shirt. She bent her legs at an impossibly wide angle that had his cock practically fucking her to get it off. He groaned as she bared him and whispered, "Minx," against her mouth when he took it back. As they kissed, he tugged at her t-shirt.

Carmen was reduced to panting and moaning his name, receiving his kisses, and offering herself. She raised her arms so he could pull the t-shirt off. But Ramiro stopped as it was halfway up her arms. As she stared at him in confusion, his green eyes twinkled, and he pressed his hands on her trapped arms, telling her they were to remain like this with a quick incline of his head. She bit her lip and watched as his pupils enlarged at the sight of her naked chest, the slight mounds of her breasts, and the star piercing that framed her aureoles held by studs threaded through her nipples.

Her breasts swelled under Ramiro's scrutiny. When he flicked his tongue around one nipple, she wailed.

He stopped and looked at her. "Sensitive?"

She shook her head wildly. "Keep going," she gasped.

He grinned and nuzzled the area between her breasts. "God, I've wanted to see these again. I had no idea. Fucking had no idea," he said before wrapping his lips around her nipple again. He sucked loudly, drawing another cry from her. She struggled to free her arms, writhing and squirming, and Ramiro put a hand over them to stop her.

"No. Stay like that." He winked at her. "If you touch me anymore I'm going to embarrass myself. Do you have any idea how intoxicating you taste? It's steel," he placed a tender kiss on her nipple. "Steel and woman."

Then without warning, he hooked his fingers in her underwear and yanked them down. "I thought you didn't wear these," he continued, amused at her blush. "You disappoint me, minx."

"I wear panties," she retorted as she dragged them down her legs before flinging them away. He elbowed her legs open and grinned at her. "Sometimes I just skip them. Oh. *God.*" She moaned as Ramiro pressed his tongue on her clit.

He kissed and licked her, heightening the rising tension in her body. Then he tortured her some more when his fingers fucked her. They were sharp, deep thrusts in her cunt, curling and turning. Too much. *Too good.* She curled her legs, but Ramiro grunted and flattened his palms on her thighs, spreading her wider. He sucked on her clit hungrily, and his fingers fucked her vigorously. She couldn't tell if the sounds she was hearing were his wet kisses or the deep forays of his fingers inside her. She looked into his eyes before she had to look away, unable to take the intensity beaming from his gaze. A few strokes, a few more turns of his tongue on her clit, and she shattered, her cry piercing the quiet of the morning.

She was still shaking from her orgasm, her vision washed with golden stars when she felt Ramiro's lips back on her. She blushed as she tasted the bittersweet tang of her cunt from his tongue and blushed even more, when she managed to free her arms from the t-shirt to cup his face so she could suck on his tongue. He purred against her lips, and she giggled. Then she started touching him again.

"Minx," Ramiro licked her lips,a pleading note entering his voice. "Maybe don't touch me so much. I haven't fucked in over a year. I want to make this last, make this good for us."

As his lips resumed kissing her breasts, Carmen's ardor began to thaw, replaced by the stubborn return of sense. Oh god. They were going to fuck.

She was his manager! They were friends!

Not when they fucked.

Oblivious to the change in her mood, Ramiro turned his head to suck on her other nipple, his fingers pinching and plucking at the one he had just left. "I knew you'd be sweet."

"Ramiro." She said, her voice sounding disembodied. "Ramiro. Ramiro. Stop. Please, stop."

She must have sounded afraid because he immediately pulled away. He sat back on his heels, and she wrestled the shirt back on. Her breasts were heavy with arousal, and her nipples were worse, tight, and painful at the interruption. Ramiro rolled to the side, and she caught a glimpse of his cock, golden and erect. Blushing, she rose from the bed.

"This was a mistake," she managed to say, hugging herself to hide her traitorous nipples. Tugging the t-shirt to hide her cunt was useless because it was too short.

Ramiro looked disgruntled as he covered himself with a sheet. He rubbed his eyes and sighed loudly. "You're right. You're engaged. I'm sorry."

"No. Tanner and I are over."

He looked at her, surprised. "Since when?"

"Last night. Just last night. Ramiro, no. We can't do this."

"I understand. You need time. I should have - "

"No." She shook her head vehemently. "Never. We can't. We shouldn't. Not in a month, not a year from now. Never."

Ramiro stared at her, frowning. "And why is that?"

"Because we have a good relationship. What we have works. I'm your manager. We're friends. Let's not screw it up."

"What the hell makes you think that fucking would be a mistake?" Ramiro demanded. He stared longingly at her bare legs. His eyes rested on the wet juncture between her thighs, brightening as she quickly palmed the dark blond curls. Carmen wished desperately for a robe, though she wanted nothing more than to wrap herself around him. "Because I have no intention of stopping to fuck you once I've fucked you, Carmen. I want to fuck you. I dream of fucking you - "

His words were making her hot. She stomped her foot and shouted, "No!"

"Why? Give me a good reason."

"What happens when things end badly? We won't be able to work together again."

"Why are you so sure that's what would happen?"

"Please, Ramiro. We can't. You want to return to music. So do I. We're best for each other as we are. Until here.' She used her hands to gesture to the demarcation line and then covered herself again. "We can't. We shouldn't. We're going to ruin each other, and I'll never forgive myself if you start retaking drugs. Or worse."

The stare Ramiro threw at her rendered all warmth in the room to vanish.

"If you have so little faith in me, Carmen. You leave me no choice." He said. "You're fired. Come back to me when you're ready to face the truth."

It wasn't until a year later that Carmen showed up on Ramiro's doorstep. A lonely year for both of them though neither would have admitted it. Before she could open her mouth to say anything, she was immediately swept off her feet by the man she loved – who loved her back.

The End

This book is a Prequel to The Greatest Gift.

Book 2 of the Series

The Greatest Gift – Get it here

Reviews

5.0 OUT OF 5 STARS ♡ ♠ ♡

Reviewed in the United States on November 28, 2019

This is such a Sweet story!

The writing draws you in and keeps you involved throughout the whole story, I found myself in love with not only the characters but also the world that was created.

THE DESCRIPTIONS OF THE CHARACTERS AND THEIR FEELINGS ARE SO involved, you can truly picture it in your mind. Their attitudes toward the events that are happening makes the story even richer.

5.0 OUT OF 5 STARS **ROCK TO POP .. THE GREATEST GIFT**

Reviewed in the United States on November 11, 2019

Ramiro Brandt is a rock musician of the Seismic group turned into pop musicians going on his own. Carmen is his manager and girlfriend. They hit it off since day one, always together. But durning on of his interviews on television he announced if his song hits number one he'll sing his song on television nude!

Carmen didn't take that too well, not as a girlfriend nor as a manager.

This story is well written and the writer is amazing! You'll love the characters, the attraction these two make sends off heat wave! Get your book, its a must read!

5.0 OUT OF 5 STARS **ANOTHER GREAT READ FROM THIS TALENTED AUTHOR.**

Reviewed in the United States on November 10, 2019

I just pray all the typos, grammatical errors etc were sorted before release. Never needed to gripe before with this author's books, but as you can see from my 5 star review it might possibly have had more stars if that were possible! I confess to falling big time for the quirky main characters, their complexities & flaws, their off the charts sexual chemistry. Okay always been a fan of rock stars but I was charmed by the way this rock god fell big time for his not so stunning girl-friend/manager but it clearly worked for him & it gives me hope. He was HOT, she wasn't but she was his siren he couldn't resist. Did I mention this was HOT?

5.0 OUT OF 5 STARS **THE GREATEST GIFT**

Reviewed in the United States on November 14, 2019

An engaging story line that pulls you in and keeps your attention til the end. The banter between the characters is great and they feel like part of your family when you finish the book. Another great one from Jennifer!

5.0 OUT OF 5 STARS **LOVED THIS BOOK**

Reviewed in the United States on November 10, 2019

Another great read from this author. I loved the characters in this one. I could really connect with them. I didn`t find any plot holes at all or even any spelling mistakes. I really connected with this story from start to finish. I was happy to read this book.

I will definitely be reading more books by this author in the future.

5.0 OUT OF 5 STARS **GREAT STORY FROM BEGINNING TO END**

Reviewed in the United States on November 10, 2019

Carmen and Ramiro have a story to end all stories with a great group of "supporting actors/actresses" that will be forever in your mind after reading their story. I'd love to see some of these characters get their own story. Without giving away the story trust when i say the heat, laughter, love, family dynamics, etc will leave you on the edge of your seat.

Enjoy!! I know I did

THE GREATEST GIFT - CHAPTER 1

T he day seemed to be without end. Having wild and passionate sex for three hours last night meant they were only able to sleep for a few hours before the alarm was rudely ringing. The morning show was the last for now, as well as his performance there. Then it was off to four radio stations for interviews. Ramiro would have a few hours' rest after that before getting ready for another show. Being a musician was harder work that one could imagine, but everything he did was crucial for his comeback after his absence from the scene.

Press tours were his least favorite part about the job. They were tedious and monotonous, with the same questions, the same studio. The same headphones when in radio stations. He changed out of his suit after another morning show - he couldn't remember what it was - into a worn black t-shirt, black bomber jacket, jeans, and sneakers for the upcoming radio interviews. His girlfriend and manager, Carmen too, was dressed casually in a thick purple sweater that brought out the blue of her eyes, jeans, and dark brown boots.

After two radio shows, Ramiro was struggling with yawning. Carmen got him coffee, double-shot espresso, so he could soldier through the last show before taking a break for the One Night Show much later tonight.

The limo pulled up at the radio station, with Ramiro feeling very alert and excited. Partly due to coffee, partly for the show. It was Hardtone with Drak Attack, the only decent radio show around that devoted two hours to rock music. Carmen cautioned Ramiro that he was likely to get attacked for his recent choices.

"Good afternoon and welcome to Hardtone with Drak Attack," came the smooth, raspy voice of Drak Attinson. He was tall, handsome with black hair and navy blue eyes. "Today's guest has recently undergone an interesting career shift, and we, the gods of rock, are here to question the God himself. Ramiro Brandt in the house!"

Recorded applause and cheers played through the waves. Ramiro's stare was calm as Drak readied to interrogate him. He actually rubbed his palms together.

"Explain yourself!" He demanded with a boisterous laugh.

"Wild beasts don't answer to orders," Ramiro drawled. From behind the booth, Carmen crossed her arms tightly on her chest.

"We thought you lost your balls somewhere, Ramiro," Drak said. "Alright. You have this new song out and, wait for it, it's not rock! It's pop! What the hell, man?"

Ramiro met Carmen's stare. He was looking at her past Drak's broad frame. "I sense a question somewhere there."

"You're doing a remake of a song so bad it's actually good. Why?"

"As I've been saying, artists should constantly evolve. That means experimenting. You have to open yourself to new ideas, new ways of doing things. Else you and your talent get stagnant."

"Do you mean to say Seismic is over?"

"If we are, you'd be the first to know."

"What do they have to say about this betrayal?"

"I owe a lot of things to Seismic. Let's make that clear. But we respect each other's individuality and choices. Euan is in a reality show - "

"A travesty to rock bands!"

"-and he appears to enjoy mentoring the kids. We're off doing our own things. We're a group, but we're still separate."

Ramiro was familiar with Drak's style. He was brash and rude, delivering comments and questions in ways meant to incite and provoke. Despite the coffee, he was calm, almost Zen-like. He smiled as Drak frowned.

"When is Seismic getting back together?"

"You know, I can't really answer that for now. What I can tell you more about is my current single. It's out, and I hope people like it."

"Only philistines like it."

"I don't think we should antagonize people just because they have different tastes."

"The God has spoken," Drak said mockingly.

"Well," Ramiro shrugged benignly.

"Alright. I'll ask about that song, Ramiro. What were you thinking? That's the question in everyone's mind. You're the rock god. If that old man Shane Garcia goes, the torch is passed to you. Why did you do this?"

"First, as flattering as it is to be considered as someone second to Shane Garcia, I don't see myself as such. He will always be the god, no matter what. I'm honored people think like that, but there are others just as good, even better. As to why I did this song, again, it's all about trying new things. I am categorically denying that rock music is dead. What I would like to say in response to your question is I want to make a comeback. I did things that made people hesitant in making deals with me. I understand. This is the only choice available to me. I took it. I'd like to think I made the best of it, but you be the judge."

He fought back a smirk at Drak's dumbfounded expression. He was expecting Ramiro to explode. He nodded and scrambled for something to say. "Uh, okay. That's well said."

"I'd like to take this opportunity to remind everyone that every download and purchase of the single goes to Belden County Children's Fund. Christmas is in four weeks. Let's do more than our share for the children by giving them a happy Christmas."

An hour before the next show, Ramiro was in the green room getting ready. He wore a black shirt to go with the pale gray suit. Right now, tissue was tucked around the collar as make-up was applied to him.

"Pixie, when you hired this young man for tonight, were you thinking of me or yourself?" He joked as the primer was put on his face.

"He's joking," Carmen told the make-up artist. "His name is Doug. He usually does make-up for horror films."

"Really," Ramiro grinned at him. "Will you be putting fake blood on me? Fangs? Eyeballs hanging out?"

Doug chuckled. "If you want."

"Don't give him ideas," Carmen said, getting back to the magazine she was reading.

"So, you're singing tonight?" Doug asked Ramiro.

"Unfortunately," Ramiro answered.

"It's a nice version," Doug remarked. "It's my favorite song."

"Aw, man. You shouldn't have told me that." Ramiro pretended to complain, drawing a laugh from him.

Carmen grinned and crossed her legs as she flipped a page on the magazine. Though Ramiro was sitting back, it didn't escape his notice the way Doug gave her legs a look. She was wearing a long-sleeved black dress with a high neckline and a skirt inches above the knee. It was a demure dress until she turned around to show off her bare back. But the clear highlight was her legs, endless, ivory pins scattered with pink freckles. Ramiro frowned, and Doug turned back to him.

"Don't frown, or the make-up will be uneven."

Carmen, blissfully unaware of what was going on, continued to read. She would glance at them from time to time.

Doug worked quickly and efficiently. He had plucked some stray hairs between Ramiro's brows and kept the make-up minimal instead of piling it on. When he finished, it was fifteen minutes before Ramiro was to go on. Doug was to stay for touch-ups.

Done, he excused himself and asked if he could go out for a cigarette. Carmen nodded. There was still time. She was still reading when the door closed, reading some more so she didn't notice right away that Ramiro was standing and glowering at her.

"What's wrong?" She asked.

Ramiro glared at the door. "Is he gay or straight?"

Confused, she demanded, "Does it matter?"

"I don't like the way he was staring at your legs."

"How sure are you it was my legs? For all we know, it could be my shoes."

"Oh." Ramiro gave her an apologetic kiss and sat down beside her.

"You okay?" Carmen put away the magazine and turned to him. She played with a lock of his hair.

"I can think of a much better place where I'd rather be," Ramiro then dropped his hand on her lap for emphasis. She blushed as it slipped between her thighs, his fingers brushing her curls. They groaned together. "Damn you, Carmen. You really had to pick tonight of all nights not to wear underwear. I have another show after this."

"You know I don't wear underwear," she gasped, torn between yanking his marauding fingers away and letting herself be touched by them. Her eyes widened as she squeaked when he suddenly pinched her clit. "God."

"You said, sometimes you don't."

As he spoke, he slipped to his knees before her. Carmen shook her head, looking anxiously at the door. Ramiro kissed her on the knee as he draped her legs over his shoulders.

"You'll deny me a taste?"

"Someone might come in," she whispered as he peeled her skirt back, rubbing his lips and cheeks on her inner thighs. She trembled, fingers digging in the leather seat. "Ramiro."

ABOUT THE AUTHOR

I am a contemporary romance author who loves writing emotional second chance romances that are full of love, passion, conflict, angst and all of them end in HEA ,My books are standalone full length novels.

Please feel free to subscribe to my newsletter bellow and get exclusive offers , free Bonuses as well as ability to read my newly released books for FREE.

Sign up for Jennifer's mailing List here:

Grab your FREE Copy of "Back To You " as a token of thanks

www.ingramcontent.com/pod-product-compliance
Lightning Source LLC
Chambersburg PA
CBHW060354180626
46817CB00008B/3012